MW01140451

Deception

By
Mark Stephen O'Neal

This is a work of fiction that contains imaginary names, characters, places, events, and incidents not intended to resemble any actual persons, alive or dead, places, events, or incidents. Any resemblances to people, places, events, or incidents are entirely coincidental.

Deception
All Rights Reserved
Copyright 2019 © Mark Stephen O'Neal
First Edition

This book may not be reproduced, transmitted, or stored in whole or in part by any means, including graphic, electronic, or mechanical, without the express written consent of the author/publisher, Mark O'Neal Books, except in the case of brief quotations embodied in critical articles and reviews.

TABLE OF CONTENTS

1

It was half past midnight on a chilly Friday night in October of 2017, and the food on the kitchen stove had gotten cold. Greg O'Brien was cooking dinner before his fiancée, Jennifer Mason, had called and said she had to work late. He opted to finish preparing dinner anyway and had decided to wait until she got home so that they could eat together. He subsequently fell asleep on the couch after watching television once he finished cooking, and he hadn't received a call or text from her since they had spoken several hours earlier.

He tried to ignore his growling stomach but decided to heat up a plate of chicken, rice, and green beans in the microwave instead of waiting any longer. He also tried to ignore the fact that Jennifer had been coming home late night after night for months and wondered what was really going on. She was up for a promotion at her job, and this required early mornings and late nights six days a week.

The long days and nights didn't bother him as much as the fact that he barely saw her anymore. They used to make an effort to see each other in the beginning of the relationship, when they took undergrad classes together at Clark-Atlanta University. She had become very distant, and he didn't fully understand why.

They'd had problems in their relationship in the past, like their constant disagreements about their financial problems and her initial refusal to cut back on her excessive spending, but they'd always managed to work through them. However, this time was different.

She might have thought that he wasn't paying attention to the sexy underwear she started wearing underneath her business attire on her shapely, five-foot-three frame recently, or the fact that she'd stopped wearing her engagement ring. Their relationship had lost its zeal, and they didn't know how to get it back.

He heard the lock of the front door click, and he dropped his fork on the living room table. Jennifer shut the door behind her and said nothing.

"What took you so long?" Greg asked. "I've been waiting on you for hours."

"Something came up at work that needed my full attention," Jennifer answered.

"At twelve thirty in the morning?"

She began rubbing her nose excessively and said, "My goal is to get the promotion that I've worked so hard on, Greg. When there's a problem at work, it's my job to fix it."

"You can't fix everything, Jennifer. Maybe you should work harder at fixing the problems at home."

"Love isn't going to pay the bills."

"We're in a good place now that you're not spending money like there's no tomorrow anymore."

"No, I'm in a good place, and you're nothing but a leech..."

"Some things are more important than money, baby. You used to know that."

"What happened to all that ambition you used to have, huh? We were supposed to be living the dream, but you'd rather settle for a job as a lowly shift manager at McDonalds."

"You know that I'm still studying to finish taking the CPA exam early next week, don't you? You're a damn snob."

"I'm a boss...not some grunt or peon like you. I've been extremely patient with you, Greg, but if we can't get back on the same page, maybe we should go our separate ways."

"Maybe we should go our separate ways because you're not the Jennifer I used to know."

"Pack your stuff and move out, then..."

"Just like that, huh? My name is also on the lease, or did you forget?"

"You can't afford this place by yourself. The sensible thing for you to do is move into a cheaper apartment since you hate spending money so much."

"You can't afford it, either. You need to stop living beyond your means."

"I'll be just fine with my new salary once I get my promotion. You're content with cooking burgers and fries for a living and making a measly twenty-five grand."

"You act like I'm some bum sitting around and doing nothing, Jennifer. I'm sticking to my plan whether you like it or not."

"Your plan is taking forever. You've been studying and taking the CPA exam for almost two years now, and it took you six years and two schools to finish undergrad. Hell, I would've had my Ph.D. by now if I were you."

"Remind me to never tell you anything ever again—all you do is throw stuff back in my face whenever you get the opportunity. Look, I don't have rich grandparents footing the bill for me like you did—having a full class load and working full-time ain't easy, sweetheart."

"You're such a damn loser—you already failed half of the test once. Why are you gonna waste your time studying for it again?"

"I'm not a loser, and I'm not giving up, either. Did you forget that I've passed two parts of the test already? I couldn't care less if you don't believe in me."

"Let's keep it real—you barely passed the two easiest parts of the exam with a 76 and 77. The REG and AUD separate the men and women from the boys and girls."

"I will do just fine, if you must know, and nothing about that exam is easy."

"No, you're just slow. I have two sorority sisters who passed it on the first try."

"I'm not slow—fifty percent of the people who take the exam fail on the first try."

"Stop making excuses, Greg…"

"Whatever."

"Loser!"

Jennifer motioned toward their bedroom before saying, "I don't want to continue this relationship anymore."

"Is there someone else keeping you out late every night? Come on, Jennifer, I'm not blind."

"That's none of your concern."

"The hell it isn't. Come on, keep it real with me."

"Yes, there is someone keeping me occupied every night."

"Who is he?"

"He's more of a man than you'll ever be."

"That's not telling me anything…"

"I'm going to take a shower."

"No, you're not. We need to finish this conversation."

"As far as I'm concerned, the conversation is over. You can do whatever you want to do because I have to get up in a few hours."

Jennifer went upstairs, and Greg continued to sit on the couch in disgust before pounding his fist on the living room table. He'd gotten burned once again by a woman he loved and was tired of being disrespected.

He then quickly packed an overnight bag while she was in the shower and left their apartment. He saw that her shiny black 2018 BMW was parked next to his car—a midnight blue 2015 Nissan Altima—when he went downstairs to the parking lot located on the ground floor of the complex. He had noticed a gradual change in Jennifer's behavior and was willing to work through the storm of their relationship; but he couldn't tolerate the secrets, the cheating, or the disrespect. He didn't want to spend another night in that apartment, so he decided to call his sister Jessica to see if he could crash at her place. Jessica answered her phone on the third ring.

"Hello," Jessica said wearily.

"Sorry I woke you," Greg said. "I need a place to stay for a while."

"Is everything all right?"

"No, Jennifer and I broke up. I just found out that she's cheating on me."

"Damn, I'm so sorry to hear that, Greg. Sure, you can stay with me as long as you want."

"Thanks, sis. I'll be there in a few minutes."

"Okay, bye."

Greg ended the call and left the parking lot of the complex. Jessica O'Brien was his older sister by eleven months and always reminded him of that fact. She'd graduated from Spelman College with a degree in communications and landed a job with the hottest radio station in town after interning there for a summer.

Jessica lived only a few minutes away, so he decided to stop at McDonald's. He hadn't finished the dinner that he'd cooked and was still hungry.

The lights inside of McDonald's and the sign were off, and he looked at his watch and saw that it was already after one o'clock. He sighed and proceeded to continue in the direction of Jessica's place, which was in the Emory Village area, and she was sitting by the front window of her apartment when he parked in the lot.

Jessica was a slim and shapely five-foot-nine caramel beauty who looked more like a Victoria's Secret model than a popular local radio personality. She buzzed him in, and he walked briskly toward her apartment door on the first floor of the complex.

"Hey," she said, as she stood in the cracked door frame.

"Hey, sis," he said. "Thanks for letting me crash here."

"You're welcome. Wanna talk about it?"

"No, thanks. Don't you have to get up in the morning?"

"Nope, I'm off from the station on weekends, remember?"

"Oh, yeah, that's right. I must have mistaken you for my ex-fiancée...she seems to work every day of the week."

"What's her deal, Greg? I saw her out with her sorority sisters at the Hard Rock Café a few weeks ago, but she didn't even acknowledge me when I spoke to her."

"I wish I had an answer for you, but I don't. She's not the same girl I used to know."

"She had us all fooled with the nice girl act. I'm so glad I didn't pledge Sigma at Spelman because I would've had to break bread with her and her snotty soros."

"She called me slow because I failed half of the CPA exam the first time—I graduated with a 3.3 GPA in accounting, so I'm far from being dumb. And to add insult to injury, she called me a loser and said her lover was more of a man than I would ever be. I can't believe she said that garbage to me."

"You're not dumb or a loser, Greg, so don't even sweat that. She's just trying to push your buttons, that's all."

"I know, but it still hurts just the same."

"Don't worry about her. You can stay here as long as you need to. Besides, you wouldn't be cramping my style, because I don't have a man these days."

"What you got going on this weekend?" he asked, changing the subject.

"I have a promotion party to do at that new club in Buckhead," she answered. "Everybody who's somebody is gonna be there."

"I guess I'll just chill and watch Netflix."

"That sounds boring—you should come to the party."

"Thanks, but no thanks. I wouldn't know how to fit in at a party like that."

"Rosalyn will be there."

"So what?"

"We've really gotten close again in the last year since we've been during the morning show together, and she really misses you."

"I'm never going down that road again, Jessie, and besides that, what happened to the real estate guy?"

"His name is Bill."

"Whatever."

"She broke it off with him because he wanted to marry her, but she didn't feel the same way."

"Well, at least she was honest with him."

"Yep, you can always count on Roz's honesty."

"You got anything to eat?" he asked, putting an end to the Rosalyn conversation. "I didn't get a chance to finish the food I cooked for Jennifer and me."

"You cooked? Since when?"

"Tonight. I may not be able to burn like you or Mom, but I can cook."

"You can't even boil an egg...no wonder Jennifer came home late. She was trying to avoid your cooking."

"Whatever."

"Look in the fridge...I have some leftover Hamburger Helper, and you're welcome to it."

"Thanks."

"Clean up when you're done. I'm going back to bed."

"I got you."

"There are some sheets and a comforter in the linen closet. You'll have to make up the bed in the guest room yourself."

"No problem, and once again, thanks for everything, sis."

"That's what family's for. Good night."

"See you in the morning."

Greg warmed the food up in the microwave while Jessica went back to bed. He then took off his jacket and plopped down on the living room sofa, and he grabbed the remote and turned on the television. He sighed and rubbed his head while flicking channels, and he found *Fast & Furious 6* before the microwave stopped. He had to settle for a wind down with Vin Diesel instead of the hot and passionate sex he craved from his now-ex-fiancée, Jennifer.

2

Horace Shingles was up bright and early on Saturday morning still on a high from landing a position at Shingles, Johnson, and Williams—his father's prestigious law firm in Manhattan. He had just finished the law school program at Harvard and passed the bar exam on the first try. Sasha Mays, his soon-to-be wife, was still asleep from a long, stressful week of work as a software developer and from planning the last-minute details of their wedding. Horace had also given her a workout with some wild, passionate sex before they were both completely comatose several hours earlier. She had the life that she always wanted and was marrying her soulmate, but the stress of the big event was taking a toll on her. Their wedding was in two weeks, and nearly everyone had responded to the invitations.

They represented the archetypal couple of the millennium—he was tall, dark, and handsome; and she was a statuesque six-foot, light-brown-complected beauty who command attention whenever she stepped foot inside a room. They were envy of all their peers as every one of them strove to reach their level careerwise and relationship wise.

He decided to cook breakfast and bring it to her in bed. The aroma of bacon, scrambled eggs, and grits aroused her senses and woke her up from her deep sleep.

"Good morning, baby," he said. "I cooked you breakfast."

"It smells so good, and I'm starving," she said.

"I cooked plenty…eat as much as you want."

"You really wore me out last night, baby. Thank you for relieving my stress."

"You're welcome…anything for my boo."

She took a bite of her bacon and said, "Nearly everyone responded to the invitations. I hope nothing goes wrong."

"Everything will be perfect…you'll see."

"Did Greg get his tux yet?"

"I don't know. He said he picked out the one he was going to buy last week and sent me a picture of it when he was at the store, but he didn't confirm that he bought it yet."

"I'm sure that he did. What about Jennifer?"

"He didn't say anything about her. They're still not talking much these days."

"They're still having problems, huh?"

"Yeah, Jennifer is very distant, and Greg doesn't know why."

"Do you think she's cheating on him?"

"I can't say…he suspects that she might be."

"That's so messed up. I thought they'd be married before us."

"I know. They used to be so happy, but she makes a lot more money than he does."

"So, it was all about the money?"

"I truly believe so. Greg always complained about Jennifer's spending habits once she landed her first job after graduation."

"It shouldn't just be about the money. I'd marry you even if you didn't have a dime. I love you."

"I love you, too, Sasha."

Horace paused and said, "Aren't you glad we decided to wait instead of getting married right after leaving Clark?"

"Yes, baby, it was definitely worth the wait because I'm having the wedding of my dreams. Our budget wouldn't have allowed us to plan the wedding that I wanted if we had gotten married right after undergrad. Your dad is a godsend."

"Yes, I'm glad he's paying for it…a graduation gift, if you will. I'm just happy you're getting the wedding you want and deserve, sweetheart."

"Thanks to you, I am."

Sasha continued to eat her food while Horace went to the kitchen to fix his plate. He came back to their bedroom with his plate and two glasses of orange juice.

"Do you know why Ramona doesn't want to be in the wedding?" he asked. "She should be in it because you two are more than just cousins, you're sisters."

"You're right; we are sisters, but I don't have time to focus on the fact that she's not going to be in our wedding."

"Is she even coming?"

"I don't know…she still hasn't confirmed her invitation."

"What's wrong with her? She's not that busy."

"We're not as close as we used to be, baby. Something is going on with her, and she hasn't shared it with me yet."

"I think she's jealous of our relationship. She can't stand the fact that you have something great, and she still sleeps around with every guy in town."

"That's not fair, Horace. She lost her mom at an early age, and maybe that was her way of coping with it."

"Don't make excuses for her…she's supposed to be there for you, but she's being selfish instead."

"Let's agree to disagree on this."

"It's a good thing you and Roz are still close," he said. "I really appreciate her flying out here to help you plan our wedding. She's been great."

"Yes, she has. I don't know what I would've done without her."

"She's not the same, selfish person I used to know. I definitely like the person she's become."

"She's definitely not the same…she wears her success well."

"Yeah, Roz and Jessica's joint is one of the hottest shows in the country."

"Do you think Greg will ever get back together with Roz now that his relationship with Jennifer is on the rocks?"

"I doubt it. When she hooked up with that guy Dave, it really messed him up. I didn't think he'd ever get over her, but Jennifer helped him get through it."

"I guess Jennifer was good for something."

"What's up? You two aren't getting along?"

"No, not since I told her that Roz was going to be my maid of honor. I guess she took offense to that."

"Did she confirm her invitation?"

"Nope, and I can't worry about that, either. I can't trip on her being a jerk."

"Yeah, you can't let either one of them stress you out."

"I'm trying, but I'm losing that battle."

"Let me lighten your load…if there's anything you need, please let me know."

"You've been great, and I'm fine, Horace. I just wish I could relax today even though I know that I can't."

"What you got going on today?"

"I have to meet with the wedding planner about the guest list, the menu, and a few other things, and my truck needs servicing…"

"Say no more. I'll take your truck to the shop."

"Oh no, baby, I don't want to trouble you. I know you have stuff to do."

"I'm straight…don't worry about that. I got you."

"Okay. So, are you excited about working for your father?"

"It's a dream come true, and I don't want to let him down."

"You won't."

"So, how was your last day at work?"

"My boss threw me a going-away party, and everyone signed a card for me."

"Sounds nice. I know you're sacrificing a lot to move to New York, because I know how much your job meant to you."

"Yes, I loved my job, but I'll find another one."

"I know you will, babe."

He took a sip of his juice and said, "Are we taking our furniture with us to New York? I can call the movers today and set something up."

"I don't know yet…I might decide to donate it to charity, because I think I want new furniture in our new place."

"Good idea. When is our apartment going to be ready?"

"It should be ready by the time we come back from our honeymoon. Our view overlooks Central Park"

"You picked a great location. I also think that you have a second career as an interior decorator."

"You really think so?"

"No doubt. You're a woman of many talents."

"You really know how to stroke a girl's ego," she said before she leaned in for a kiss. "You'd better stop it before you spoil me rotten."

"That's the idea. There's nothing I wouldn't do to make you happy."

Sasha got up and placed her plate on the nightstand that housed a lamp next to the bed and said, "Thank you for breakfast in bed."

"Loving you is so easy, Sasha," he said. "This is how it's gonna be for the rest of our lives."

"You make me so happy. I love you."

"I love you more."

"I need to tell you something, baby," Sasha said abruptly.

"What is it, sweetheart?" Horace asked.

"I need to catch a flight to Atlanta today."

"Why?"

"It's Ramona. I haven't heard from her in weeks, and I'm worried about her."

"What about your meeting with the wedding planner?"

"I can reschedule the meeting with her on Monday or Tuesday."

"Come on, Sasha, Ramona is all right. I think you're jumping the gun by booking a flight to Atlanta today."

"I can't shake this feeling I have, Horace. I really need to see my cousin and make sure she's okay. I won't be able to relax until I know what's going on with her."

"Okay, I understand. I'll hold it down here while you see about Ramona."

"Thank you for understanding."

"No need to thank me…I'd do anything for you."

"I love you, Horace," Sasha said as she leaned in for another kiss.

"I love you, too," Horace said after their long, passionate kiss. Let's get ready to go…I'll drive you to the airport before I take your truck to the dealership."

"All right, you shower first. I'll book my flight right now."

3

Jennifer awakened from her deep sleep and let off a few choice expletives when she discovered that it was well after nine o'clock. She slowly climbed out of bed and checked her caramel-complected face in the mirror of her dresser before tracing the dark circles around her eyes with her index finger and sighing in disgust. Her entire body ached as she crept to the bathroom, and she reached inside of her purse, which was hanging on the bathroom door, and grabbed a small vial. She then emptied its contents onto the tip of her index finger and snorted them.

She was fully alert and dressed about ten minutes later, and she walked briskly to her car once she reached the lower-level parking lot. Her phone rang before she could shut the driver side door.

"I'm on my way," she said.

"We need to talk about your position on Bailey Morton potentially acquiring Greenwood," her boss said. "Our client has a lot riding on this deal."

"Like I said before, I stand firm on my position."

"So, you don't recommend that they make the deal?"

"No, they shouldn't make the deal because there's no profit in check processing…at least not the kind of profit that they're used to making in this current economy. They be lucky to break even in the first five years."

"The firm believes that the industry has merely transformed, not become extinct. Yes, people aren't writing as many checks these days, but they still believe Bailey Morton can still make a significant profit by acquiring Greenwood and laying off half of their workforce."

"I'm sorry, Marcus, I can't side with the firm on this one, and I won't try to paint a pretty picture by being creative with the numbers and telling our client what he wants to hear."

"Are you sure? Because both of our futures may hinge on this deal, Jennifer."

"Why is that, Marcus?"

"Let me be the first to tell you that you're up for a promotion and significant raise as a senior financial analysis, which is contingent on the Bailey Morton-Greenwood deal."

"Really?! Oh, wow!"

"Calm down, sweetheart…I'm not even supposed to be leaking this info to you."

"I won't say a word…I promise."

"So, you're confident in your decision?"

"Yes, baby, I am. I've gone over the numbers repeatedly, and my final analysis was always the same."

"Well, I trust that you know what you're doing."

There was a brief silence, and Marcus said, "Are you wearing that sexy underwear I love so much?"

"Down, boy—business before pleasure, remember?"

"I can't help it, Jennifer. I want you every night—I need you every night, but we have to make the most of our few stolen moments."

"We don't have to sneak around anymore."

"What are you telling me?"

"Greg pack his bags and left after I told him what was going on."

"He knows about us?"

"Not exactly. I told him that there was someone else, but he doesn't know it's you."

"That's great, baby. Let's skip work today and go straight to the hotel."

"No, I think we really need to reevaluate our relationship."

"Reevaluate our relationship? What is there to reevaluate?"

"Greg is out of the picture, Marcus. Now, are you going to leave your wife for me?"

"Baby, we've already been through this…"

"Been through what? So, I can give up my relationship, but you can't give up yours?"

"I have kids…I have a family. I can't just walk away from them."

"What about me?"

"I love you, Jennifer, but I can't leave my family right now."

"But you don't love me enough to be with me full-time."

"Come on. Don't be like that."

"Goodbye, Marcus."

"Wait…"

"What?"

"Are we still meeting each other at Starbucks?"

"What do you think?"

Jennifer disconnected the call and tossed her phone on the passenger side seat. She listened as Marcus tried to call back several times but eventually gave up. She then decided to dine without Marcus at one of her favorite breakfast spots nearby her place.

Phase two of her plan was now in full effect. She was determined to have Marcus all to herself and live the great life that she craved—even if it meant destroying a family to get what she wanted.

"Call Pam," she instructed the voice command of her iPhone to dial.

"Hey, girl," Pamela said. "What's going on?"

"Can you meet me at Rise-N-Dine?" Jennifer asked.

"Yeah, give me a few minutes to get ready, and I'll meet you there."

"Okay, see you there."

"Jennifer…"

"What is it?"

"Is everything okay?"

"We'll talk about it when you get here."

"All right."

Jennifer disconnected the call and continued in the direction of the restaurant. She arrived there several minutes later and parked on the side of the restaurant on North Decatur Road in Emory Village, and waited for Pamela. The chocolate beauty arrived thirty minutes later and spotted Jennifer's car as she had parked in a space that was toward the end of the block. Her hips swayed from side to side as she strutted in the direction where Jennifer was waiting, and Jennifer hopped out of her car to hug Pamela.

"What's up, girl?" Pamela asked.

"I'm going through some stuff, and I need to talk to you about it," Jennifer answered.

"Let's go inside and get a table."

They stepped inside and the hostess promptly seated them. The waitress walked over to their table a minute later.

"Good morning. My name is Cindy, and I'll be your server today."

"Good morning," Pam said, and Jennifer said nothing.

"Can I get you all anything to drink?" Cindy asked.

"I'll have a coffee," Pamela said.

"Coffee," Jennifer added curtly.

"Coming right up," Cindy said before she walked away.

"Thank you," Pamela said. "What's your deal, Jen? You didn't have to be rude to that girl."

"I don't give a damn about her," Jennifer answered. "I came here because I need my friend…the only true friend I have left."

"What's wrong?"

"Greg and I broke up."

"Why?"

"I'm not feelin' him anymore. We're just not on the same page."

"Did he cheat on you?"

"No, I'm cheating on him."

"Jennifer, what the hell is wrong with you?"

"Nothing is wrong with me."

"Greg is a great guy…I don't understand why you're dogging him out like this."

"So, you're going to take his side without hearing mine?"

"What was so bad that it made you step out on him?"

"He's not ambitious enough for me. He's hellbent on working at McDonald's until he passes the CPA exam."

"And what's wrong with that?"

"I think he's wasting his time. He already failed the test miserably the first time, and I just don't think he's smart enough to pass it."

"So, maybe he had a bad day the first time he took the test. Everybody has a bad day every now and then."

"That may be, but why can't he get a better job in the meantime so that he can help me out more?"

"I hear what you're saying, Jen, but life isn't always that simple. Maybe he's comfortable where he is at the moment, and I'm sure Greg has a plan and will make it work for himself eventually."

"Who are you, his cheerleader? I want it all, Pam, and I'm not going to wait another five years for him to step up. An ordinary life just isn't good enough for me anymore, and I won't settle for less."

"Jennifer, you're talking real stupid. I'm your girl, so I'm gonna give it to you straight. You're really messing up your life right now."

Cindy brought their coffee and said, "Are you ready to order?"

"Not yet!" Jennifer abruptly shouted.

"Okay, I'll give you a few minutes to decide," Cindy said before quickly walking away.

"Messing up my life?" Jennifer asked. "Who the hell are you to judge me?"

"I'm not judging you," Pamela answered. "I'm just calling it like I see it. If you can't handle the truth, you shouldn't have shared your story with me."

"I wanted you to listen, not give me a lecture."

"I wouldn't be a real friend if I didn't tell you the truth…"

"You don't live with the man—you don't go through what I go through with him every day."

"You're right; I don't know what you go through with him on a daily basis. What I do know is you don't throw away a relationship just because you have a disagreement."

"Whatever, Pam. Our problem is much more than a difference in opinion—Greg has no class."

"So, you think you're better than him?"

"I'm not saying that exactly…"

"So, who's the mystery guy you've been creeping with?" Pam asked, changing the subject.

"He's my boss, and he's also married."

"What?! Have you lost your damn mind?"

"He's going to leave his wife for me real soon. We're in love."

"I can't believe that you're okay with being a homewrecker. Who is this person sitting across from me?"

"You know what…go to hell, Pam!"

"You're really going talk to me like that after all we've been through?"

"Yes, Pam, I am. You can leave now because I have nothing more to say to you."

"Fine, then. Do me a favor and lose my number, heifer."

Pamela stormed out of the restaurant, and Jennifer sat alone in embarrassment. Cindy came back to the table to take their orders.

"Are you ready to order?" Cindy asked.

"Just bring me the bill for the coffee," Jennifer answered.

"As you wish, ma'am."

A tear rolled down her right cheek as she realized that she might have lost the only true friend she had left. She didn't believe in self-pity, so she sucked it up and checked her makeup in the camera window of her phone instead.

4

Greg woke up to the familiar aroma of the country-style breakfast that he grew up on as a youth. Jessica was a great cook like their mom, and she would often cook at the drop of a hat. Greg smiled as he entered the kitchen, and he observed that Jessica had set the table for two.

"Smells good, sis," Greg said.

"Help yourself," she said. "I cooked plenty."

He washed his hands in the sink with dishwashing liquid and grabbed a paper towel before saying, "I tossed and turned all night long. I haven't had a good night's sleep in months."

"Jennifer cut you off, huh?" she asked.

"How can you tell?"

"You would've slept well if you'd gotten some last night."

"We used to have great sex, but that all changed after she started working at that new firm."

"Where does she work again?"

"Bergman, Mitchell, & Schultz."

"That's a great firm. One of my friends interviewed with them, but she didn't get the job."

"I almost wish Jennifer didn't get the job."

"Don't be a hater. Jennifer was going to cheat on you, regardless of the circumstances, because she's disloyal. Working at Bergman, Mitchell, & Schultz merely sped up the process."

"You're probably right about that. I'm over it, though."

"Why is it that I seem to be more upset about it than you do?"

"No, I'm very upset, but I've already gone through the emotions of being full of rage and sadness and being broken-hearted. I kept everything inside with hopes of Jennifer snapping out of it and being the girl I fell in love with again."

"I think I should pay Little Miss Jennifer a visit…"

"Stay out of it, Jessie. Don't make a bad situation worse."

"Nobody disrespects my family and gets away with it, baby brother. Miss Thang has a date with my fists."

"And what is that gonna prove? Beating her up won't change anything."

"It will make me feel better. I can't stand phony people."

"Just let it go."

Greg took a bite of his Texas toast and said, "So, are you psyched about going to New York?"

"Hell, yeah...it isn't every day that a girl gets to go to the Hamptons. I'll buy my outfit sometime this weekend because I probably won't have time next week or the week after that."

"I picked out my tux and bought it last week. I'm going up there next weekend to cut up with Horace for a week before the wedding."

"Good. You deserve to have some fun after what Jennifer just did to you."

"Maybe it wasn't all her fault..."

"The hell it wasn't...what makes you think you did anything wrong?"

"I don't know. Rosalyn and I went through the same drama a few years ago. Maybe it's something that I'm doing to turn these women off."

"Let's see—you're tall, handsome, and educated—you're what every girl I know wants. So, no, I don't think it's your fault, and I'm not just saying this because you're my brother."

"Sometimes you have to show a person that you have other options, or else they'll take you for granted. Somewhere down the line, I lost sight of that fact."

"You might have a point there. Maybe you should get you some female friends to make Jennifer jealous."

"That ship has sailed, Jessie. She's not that into me anymore."

"Then do it with the next girl you get with."

"I think I'm going to try being single for a while. I need to really get to know myself because I've been in relationships nonstop since high school and haven't really had time to be alone and process everything."

"I guess I never thought of it like that. You probably do need a break."

"So, when are you flying to New York?" Greg asked, changing the subject.

"I'm booked all the way up to the day before the wedding, so I'll be in town by then," Jessica answered.

"You're really doing it big, sis. I'm so proud of you."

"Thank you, Greg, I appreciate you saying that. I wish Daddy could see me now."

"He's definitely smiling down on you from Heaven."

"He's smiling down from Heaven on both of us."

Greg's phone rang, and he sighed before picking up.

"Hey, Jennifer, what's up?" Greg asked.

"I need to know when you're going to pick up the rest of your things," Jennifer answered.

"You're kicking me out already, huh?"

"Look, I don't want to go through this with you right now."

"I'm just kidding. Where's your sense of humor?"

"Whatever, Greg. So, when are you coming by?"

"I'm going to pick up my stuff later on today."

"How late is later on?"

"I'll be there around three because I have some other business to take care of."

"All right. Make sure you leave the key on the dining room table, because I won't be there."

"That's fine. Don't forget to take my name off of the electric bill and the cable bill as soon as possible, because I'm going to look for another place the moment I get back in town."

"You're going out of town?"

"For Horace and Sasha's wedding, remember?"

"Damn, I totally forgot about the wedding..."

"You forgot? I thought Sasha was your friend."

"She was, but our friendship ended when she made Rosalyn her maid of honor instead of me."

"So, I guess I won't be seeing you at their wedding..."

"No, I suppose not."

"We also need to talk to the landlord about removing my name from the lease."

"That shouldn't be a problem. I'll set it up next week."

"Great, I'll call you when I finish packing my stuff. You can have all of the furniture, and you can keep the ring. The only two things I want that we bought together are my laptop and one of our three HD televisions."

"I don't have a problem with that, either. You can take the one in the guest room."

"Okay, that's fair."

"I just want to say that I never meant to hurt you, Greg, and I still have love for you. I'm really sorry."

"I'm not hurt, but I appreciate your apology. I saw the writing on the wall months ago and had time to prepare for it. I wish you all the best."

"Goodbye, Greg."

"Goodbye, Jennifer."

Greg disconnected the call and sighed again before taking a gulp of orange juice. Jessica shook her head and said, "That went surprisingly well. No fireworks or name-calling...I guess you've really gotten over the whole situation."

"It makes no sense to dwell on it. It's time for me to move on."

"Are you really going to let her keep the ring?"

"Yeah, I don't have any use for it, and besides, I'm not going to take back a gift that I bought her."

"You saved up for months to buy that ring."

"It's not about the money."

"You're right...it's not about the money, but she doesn't deserve to keep it. Why reward her for bad behavior?"

"I'm trying to be the bigger person in all this."

"She's counting on you being the bigger person. If I were you, I'd shake things up."

"But you're not me. I just want to put this relationship in my rearview mirror, and I don't want to hold on to any negative memories of her. Can you understand that?"

"I'm sorry, and you're right. When it's over, it's over."

"And I'm looking forward to being single for the first time in my adult life."

"Since you're going to be single, you should kick things off by coming to this party tonight."

"Maybe I will."

"It's going to start at nine. Some A-list celebs are going to be there."

"I don't trip on stuff like that. I just want to mingle and have a good time."

"And you deserve to have some fun for a change instead of working so damn hard all the time."

"You're absolutely right, Jessie. Here's to new beginnings."

Jessica raised her glass of orange juice and added, "And here's to being single. Don't knock it until you've tried it."

"Amen to that," Greg said.

5

Rosalyn Coleman had driven slowly through the Clark-Atlanta University campus en route to Ramona's apartment on Mildred Street—the same place she'd had since she had attended the school. Rosalyn's shiny red Chevy Camaro with chrome rims drew the attention of practically every student who was on the yard at that time. Ramona lived a few blocks from Clark, and driving through campus brought back memories of the not-so-distant past. She simply missed the fun times that she'd had there and wasn't trying to flaunt her success.

After taking a trip down memory lane, Rosalyn pulled up in front of Ramona's apartment and parked her car in the lot. She had hoped to catch Ramona before she left out for the day. She then rang the doorbell and got no response, so she called Ramona's cell phone.

"Hey, Roz," Ramona said.

"Are you at home?" Rosalyn asked.

"Yeah, why?"

"I'm outside. Buzz me in."

"My doorbell must not be working. I'll buzz you in now."

Rosalyn entered the building and took the elevator to the third floor. Ramona had the door cracked open when Rosalyn got there. She was still in her robe when Rosalyn stepped inside.

"Where have you been hiding, girl?" Rosalyn asked before hugging Ramona. "I haven't seen you in months."

"I haven't been feeling well lately," Ramona answered.

"Look at you—you've lost so much weight."

"I know."

"I miss you."

There was an uneasy silence for a moment, and Rosalyn asked, "Are you going to your cousin's wedding?"

"I don't know."

"What do you mean you don't know?"

"I have cancer, Roz."

"What?"

"I have stage four cervical cancer, and I don't have much time."

"Why haven't you told us? And what do you mean you don't have much time?"

"My doctor gave me six months to live, three months ago. You're the first person that I've told."

"So, Sasha doesn't know?" Rosalyn asked as her voice quivered and eyes began to tear up.

"I haven't found the right words to say to her yet," Ramona answered. "She's going to be devastated."

"I'm devastated, Mona. I can't believe you didn't share this with me sooner. I could've taken you to your treatments and everything. You robbed me of the chance to spend as much time as I could with you."

Rosalyn broke down, and Ramona put her arms around her in an attempt to comfort and calm her down. Ramona kissed Rosalyn on the forehead and said, "I'm sorry I didn't tell you sooner, Roz. I'm going through my own issues and don't want to burden anybody."

"But I'm not just anybody…"

"I know, please forgive me."

"There's nothing to forgive. I love you."

"I love you, too."

Rosalyn let go of her embrace and asked, "When is your next treatment? I want to be there for you."

"There's nothing more the doctors can do for me," Ramona answered. "The cancer is too aggressive."

"There has to be something we can do. There are alternative methods we can try, Mona. Money is no object…I'll make sure you get the best care possible."

"Thanks, but no thanks, Roz. I've come to terms with my mortality, and I'm at peace with it."

"I'm not ready to let you go."

"I know, but it's in God's hands now."

Rosalyn had begun weeping uncontrollably, and Ramona let her cry on her shoulder as she continued to comfort her. Ramona reminisced about the time Rosalyn kicked her ex-boyfriend Dave in the groin at a club, and they all ran out before the bouncers could catch them. Rosalyn had torn her dress up to her rear end from running, Sasha broke the heel of one of her stilettos, and Rosalyn and Sasha had a heated argument before everyone patched things up and hung out at Denny's restaurant until the wee hours of that morning.

"Remember when you kicked your ex Dave in the balls at that club?" Ramona asked.

"Yes, I do," Rosalyn answered, chuckling after she wiped away her tears. "If I had a knife, I would've given him the Lorena Bobbitt special."

"He definitely deserved a kick in the balls, but slicing his penis off is a bit extreme."

"All jokes aside, I reached out to him recently and apologized to him for doing that. We both did things to hurt each other, and I needed closure."

"How is he doing?"

"His business is thriving, and he's married with a newborn baby girl."

"Good for him. I'm glad you two can be civil toward one another."

"It's all part of my anger management exercise I learned from my self-help book. I have to try to make peace with everyone I've had beef with in my past."

"Like Jessica, right?"

"Especially her. We've become very close."

"She's your new BFF?"

"No one can ever replace you, Mona."

"It's okay, Roz. You're gonna need someone to lean on when I'm gone."

"Don't say that."

"It's the truth. Sasha has Horace, and you're gonna need Jessica."

"I'm not giving up on you."

"So, what happened with that guy Bill? I thought you two were getting married."

"Marrying him would've been a big mistake."

"You're still not over Greg, are you?"

"No, I'm not over him."

"Then you should do something about it."

"But what can I do? He doesn't feel the same way anymore."

"I disagree. He was hurt, and he doesn't know how to trust you again."

"What about Jennifer?"

"She was a rebound, and from what Sasha tells me, there's trouble in paradise."

"What kind of trouble?"

"She hasn't been treating Greg right, and this could be your opportunity to get him back."

"I don't want to seem desperate…"

"Closed mouths don't get fed, Roz. You'll never know unless you try."

"Maybe you're right. I'll give him a call."

"If he doesn't give you another chance, that's okay—at least you'll have the answers that you need to move forward."

"We'll see."

"You have nothing to lose."

6

Horace waited patiently at the car dealership where Sasha had bought her Honda SUV, to get it serviced. There was a college football game on that barely piqued his interest, so he dabbled on his phone instead. There was a young lady sitting next to him buried in her phone as well, and an older man sitting on the other side of him was engrossed in the game. He was shouting obscenities at the television screen, and other patrons were looking at him as if he were certifiable. Horace's phone rang, and he stepped outside to take the call.

"Hey, Dad," Horace said.

"Hey, Son," Mr. Shingles said. "Are you excited about your big day?"

"My first day at work or my wedding day?"

"Your wedding, Son. I already know you'll do fine at the firm."

"I'm a little nervous, but I'm ready."

"Sasha is a fine young lady, so you don't have anything to worry about."

"I know, Dad."

"As for your best man, I think you should go with your cousin, Richard."

"My mind is made up. Greg is going to be my best man."

"I like Greg, Horace, I really do, but I believe family should come first."

"It's my wedding, and I believe it should be my choice who the best man is, not yours."

"Let me remind you who's footing the bill…"

"I'll postpone the wedding and pay for it myself at a later date, then."

"You will do no such thing."

"I wish you would stop trying to control my life."

"I'm not trying to control your life. I only want what's best for you."

"I appreciate everything you've done for me and don't want to sound ungrateful, but I need you to back off and let me make my own decisions."

"I just want you to benefit from my years of wisdom."

"I get it, okay? Look, I have to go…"

"This discussion isn't over."

"Goodbye, Dad."

Horace abruptly ended the call and remained outside of the dealership to blow off some stream. He resented the fact that his life up to this point had been carefully crafted and orchestrated by both of his parents and wished there were a way to alleviate the pressure. Unfortunately, that day hadn't come yet.

He stepped back inside, and his seat had been taken. The girl who was sitting next to him informed him that the technician said his car was ready. He then went to the counter to pay the cashier and get his keys. The next thing on his agenda was to get a haircut and shave at a barbershop in Roxbury. He knew the owner because he had befriended him while they were in school at Clark.

Sasha's dealership was near the Harvard campus in Cambridge, so it took Horace about fifteen minutes to get to his friend's barbershop. He parked in a vacant spot off the intersection of Washington and School Street and walked inside the barbershop moments later. All seats were filled, so he would have to make an afternoon of it because the shop was packed.

"Is Raheem here?" Horace asked one of the other barbers.

"He's in the back," the guy said. "He'll be out in a minute."

"Okay," Horace said.

Raheem came out a few minutes later with some fresh towels, and he spotted Horace seated near the door. He walked over and gave Horace a pound.

"What's up, my dude?" Raheem asked.

"Everything is everything," Horace answered. "As you can see, I'm badly in need of a touch up."

"I got you. So, you ready for your big day?"

"Ready as I'll ever be. My dad is all in my business, though."

"Be happy you have a father that cares enough about you to stay in your business, because most of us don't."

"Duly noted."

"Slide over here to my chair, and I'll get you in."

"You sure? There are at least ten other people ahead of me."

"You're my boy, so don't even worry about that."

Horace sat in Raheem's chair and asked, "Are you going to make it to the wedding?"

"I wouldn't miss it for the world," Raheem answered.

"That's what's up. The bachelor party is going to be off the chain."

"I'm sure it will be."

There was an interesting dialogue amongst everybody in the shop going on, and the topic of conversation was the mass of recent cop shootings in various cities across the country. Raheem and Horace decided to join in.

"Bruthas are sick and tired of laying down to these cops," one of the patrons said. "It's time to take a stand."

"But they gotta license to shoot a brutha anytime he get outta pocket, son," another patron said. "I ain't trying to go out like that."

"The hell with that…if they mess with me, I got some heat to back me up."

"And you're gonna be one dead negro."

"What you think, Raheem?" patron number one asked. "If the cops messed with you, what would you do?"

"As much as I hate to say this, I agree with Keith, Mike," Raheem answered. "Bruthas gotta start using common sense and proceed with extreme caution, and brothers bustin' back at cops is definitely not the answer to our problems. Just chill and live to see another day."

"You might live to see another day," Mike said. "Bruthas be complying and still get shot dead. At least if I die, I'll take one of them sorry pigs with me."

"You definitely got a one-way ticket to the grave if you try to bust back at cops," Keith said.

"At least he'd die for something," one of the patrons being serviced said. "Change doesn't happen unless people are willing to die for it."

"Are you willing to die for it, Malcolm X?" Keith asked him.

"My name is George and yes, I am," he said.

George had on a white polo shirt, gray slacks, and patent leather boots that came just above the ankle, and he also had on wire frame glasses and had a gold right front tooth. He sat in a chair getting a touch up from one of the barbers. He had the aura of a lawyer, executive, or stockbroker on Wall Street.

"I'm part of an organization called CAMP," George continued, "and it's my duty to carry on the struggle for justice and equality for our people."

"What is *CAMP*?" Keith asked.

"CAMP stands for the Continued Advancement of Melanin People," George answered. "We believe that our people as a whole represent the twelve tribes of Israel spread throughout the four corners of the Earth."

"So, you're a Black Israelite?" Horace asked.

"No, but we study the Bible thoroughly," George answered.

"I see," Horace said. "You're right about change not happening unless we're ready to sacrifice greatly, but we have to be smart about it. Mouthing off at cops when approached isn't the right course of action."

"Then what do you suggest, homie?" Mike asked.

"We have to hit the powers that be where it hurts the most, and that's in their pockets," Horace answered. "The problem with us is we're not unified enough to pull it off."

"What's your solution to unify us?" Keith asked.

"We can start by putting this gang and drug culture to rest for good nationwide," Horace answered. "If we don't give the courts a reason to lock us up, the prison system won't make money off of us with slave labor anymore."

"That ain't gonna work," Mike said. "Most cats can't even earn a decent living without doing something illegal, and a brutha can't feed his family making just ten bucks an hour."

"Mike's right, dawg," Keith added. "That ain't gonna work because this system isn't designed for the average Black man to make it."

"You're not average," George interjected. "Yes, this system isn't designed for you, Black man, but the Most High has given all of you special gifts. It's up to each and every one of you to figure out what your gift is and develop it."

"Just like that, huh?" Mike asked. "You make it sound so damn easy—like the average Joe from the projects can just figure out what he's good at and make it happen."

"Our sisters are making it happen, brother," George said. "Black women are more educated than any group in the United States, and many of them come from the same projects that you're from…"

"Come on, man," Keith said, "going to school in my neighborhood was like going to a group home every day. How the hell are you supposed to learn anything in an environment like that?"

"We have to stop making excuses for ourselves," Horace said. "My parents were fortunate enough to send me to private schools, but the desire to learn comes from within. All the fancy education in the world isn't going to guarantee good grades and a high-paying job. You still have to work hard to make it happen, no matter what your circumstances are."

"Change also begins with educating our kids in a way that our parents didn't," George said. "We need to teach their kids what the school system won't."

"And who the hell has time for that?" Mike asked. "I'm dead tired after working two jobs, and I barely have time to do things around the house. Besides, I wasn't a good student anyway."

"I'm not talking about textbook stuff, my brother," George answered. "I'm talking about real-life issues…our history our and heritage. We need to arm our children with the knowledge to survive in this cold, cruel world."

"Man, I'm still trying to figure that out for my damn self," Keith said.

"We also have to empower ourselves and stop waiting for others to do it for us," Horace said. "The energy we put into selling drugs on the street is the same energy we can use to start businesses."

"And it's not just about economics or black and white," George said. "It's about the image we portray and the image of us being portrayed throughout the world. We have to carry ourselves with pride and dignity, and only then will others begin to respect us as a people. And those values are what CAMP is all about."

"Like pulling up our pants," Keith said. "Dudes act like they don't know what that truly means."

"Bruthas know what time it is, Keith," Mike said. "We ain't the only ones wearing our pants low. White and Hispanic dudes be wearing their pants low, too."

"All ya talk a good game, but let's keep it real," Raheem said. "Ain't nothing gonna change for the better because a lot of our bellies are full now. People have something to lose, unlike back in the day when our grandparents came up and didn't have a pot to piss in."

"You bring up a good point, but the struggle doesn't end just because some of our bellies are full," George said.

"Well said," Raheem said.

Raheem proceeded to cut Horace's hair and give him a shave. The conservation shifted gears, and they all started talking about the upcoming NBA season. The Celtics were the frontrunners in the Eastern Conference, and since Horace was a Knicks fan, he tuned the conversation out. Nevertheless, Raheem had Horace touched up and ready to go in a little over thirty minutes in spite of the barbershop banter.

Horace tipped Raheem and said, "I hate that you're not gonna be my regular barber anymore."

"Yeah, I'm gonna definitely miss your business," Raheem said, "but we'll still have plenty of chances to hang out in the future. I'm in the NYC quite a bit because I'm got fam there."

"No doubt. See you at the bachelor party."

They gave each other dap, and Horace left. Someone shouted Horace's name before he could open the driver side door, and he looked up and saw that it was George.

"You were real impressive in the shop," George said. "We could use a soldier like you in our organization."

"Thanks, but no thanks," Horace said.

"Very well, then. What do you do for a living?"

"I'm a lawyer, and I just passed the bar."

"Now it all makes sense. Do you have a card?"

Horace nodded before he reached in his wallet and said, "Here you go."

George took the card, read it, and asked, "What kind of law do you specialize in?"

"I specialize in criminal law," Horace answered. "My father's firm is located in downtown Manhattan."

"That's good information to know. I'm in New York a lot, so I'll give you a call if I'm ever in need of an attorney."

"Please do that. I need all the clients I can get."

"I'm sure you won't have problem building your clientele. Well, it was good talking to you…I have a flight to catch."

"Oh yeah, where are you headed?"

"I have business in Atlanta today."

"Wow, what a coincidence…my fiancée is going to Atlanta to see her cousin today."

"Yeah, it's a small world," George said, rubbing his chin. "Here, take my card—give me a call whenever you're in Boston again. Maybe we could have a drink and build one day soon."

Horace looked over his card—George Canty III, CEO, C.A.M.P. — Continued Advancement of Melanin People. He put George's business card in his pocket and asked, "What exactly to you do, George?"

"Well, I founded my youth organization to help inner-city boys age thirteen to eighteen become men," George answered. "We prepare them for college, we teach them the Bible, our history and heritage, and mathematics, and we sponsor neighborhood baseball and basketball programs for them."

"That's very impressive. I wish more people would take the initiative to make our communities better like you're doing."

"Thank you, and like I said before, the offer to join us in your spare time is always open."

"Thanks...maybe I'll take you up on that in the near future. Nice meeting you and take care."

"Peace be with you, Brother Horace."

7

The day had shaped up to be a humid one despite the fact that it was October, and Greg decided to take full advantage of it and the first taste of freedom from his breakup with Jennifer. His first order of business before getting his things from their apartment was to get his oil changed and his tires rotated. The dealership was on the other side of town, so the goal was to get there before traffic had gotten too congested.

As luck would have it, he saw Jennifer's best friend, Pamela Brown, pull up at the same time he did. However, he was in no mood for socializing, even though they had a good rapport with each other. He decided to follow her into the service area and wait for a technician to approach his vehicle rather than listen to the inner voice that told him to come back to the dealership at a later date. The technician took Pamela's keys first, and then he walked over to Greg's vehicle.

"Hello, what can we do for you today, sir?" the technician asked.

"I need an oil change and a tire rotation," Greg answered.

"What's your name?"

"Greg O'Brien."

"Let me look that up on the computer," the technician said as Greg handed him the keys to his car.

"You're due for a brake check as well," the technician said.

"Sure, go ahead," Greg said.

He walked over to the waiting area and saw Pamela buried in her phone to the left of the television that hung from the wall. He decided not to be rude and greeted her instead.

"Hey, Pam, how you doing?" he asked.

She looked up and said, "Hey, sweetie, I'm doing fine."

She stood up, and they embraced. She smiled and said, "I just bought my car from this dealership two weeks ago."

"And you need servicing already?" he asked.

"Yeah, I heard a rattling noise, so the technician told me to bring it in," she answered.

"It's good to stay on top of something like that before it becomes a bigger problem."

"I know, and we pay too much money not to take good care of our cars."

"No doubt. What year is your Maxima?"

"It's a 2017."

Pamela paused before saying, "I heard about what happened. Sorry."

"Don't be...I saw the writing on the wall months ago."

"I want you to know that I don't side with her. She's dead wrong, Greg."

"Thank you for saying that, Pam."

"If you ever want to talk about it, I'm here for you."

"Okay. Come on, let's go outside."

"We're not friends anymore, either," she said after he held the door for her.

"What?" he asked. "Since when?"

"Since today," she answered. "I told her about herself, and she didn't like it. I also told her to lose my number."

"You shouldn't have done that. She's still your friend regardless of the fact that you two had an argument. You'll patch things up...you'll see."

"I doubt it. She's not the same person I used to know."

"You're right, she definitely isn't the same person. And it's not just about her cheating on me, because something's just not right, and I can't put a finger on it."

"What are you going to do about it?"

"Nothing. She's not my problem anymore, and I'm done with the whole thing."

"Good. She's not worth it anyway."

There was a momentary silence as the two of them tried to figure out what to say next. They'd always liked each other, but neither one of them wanted to act on their mutual attraction to one another because of his relationship with Jennifer. Pamela had dated the star quarterback of the football team, named Brian Smith, from freshman year through half of junior year, but she had been single ever since their breakup at the beginning of the spring semester. Greg liked her long legs, her more-than-ample bosom and derriere, and her radiant smile; and Pamela liked the fact that Greg was tall and muscular, and she loved his kind personality. They also had a few things in common besides their taste in automobiles—they were both from Chicago, both loved the Fast and Furious saga, and both loved house music. Pamela finally broke the silence and said, "Wanna go out sometime? There's this new restaurant downtown that I'd like to try. It'll be my treat."

"I don't know if that's a good idea," he answered. "You're still Jennifer's friend..."

"*Was* Jennifer's friend. Besides, she didn't waste any time hooking up with someone. Why should you?"

"I'm not trying to hook up with anyone right now. I need time to sort things out."

"Come on. It will be fun. No strings attached, okay?"

"I'll think about it. I've always thought you were beautiful and sexy, but I'm not in the business of dating my ex's friends. Things could get real messy real fast."

"Things are already messy with Jennifer. That guy she's creeping with is her boss, and he's married with children. So you see, she doesn't care about being messy because she's a homewrecker..."

"Marcus? She's sleeping with Marcus?"

"I'm afraid so, Greg."

"Unbelievable. She invited that clown to our place with his wife for dinner not long after she started working at the firm."

"So, why should you put your life on hold? Like I said before, Jennifer certainly isn't wasting any time. I've always thought you were very handsome and sexy, too, but unlike you, I don't have any loyalty to people who aren't loyal themselves."

"Okay, you make a good point, and I hear what you're saying, but I'm not trying to go down that road with you or anybody else at this point in my life."

"I'm not trying to be tied down to anybody either because I have a full-time job and full course load in grad school. So you see, I really don't have time for a serious relationship, either."

"Jennifer told me the exact same thing before we instantly became a couple. Look, things always seem to happen too fast in my life, and I really need to slow down for a change."

"I hear you, too. We can take things as slow as you want. Besides, we're friends, and there's nothing wrong with two friends hanging out."

"Well, since you put it that way, when do you want to go out?"

"How about tonight?"

"I don't know about tonight, though. I promised my sister that I'd come to her promotion party."

"The party in Buckhead? Damn, I really wanted to go to that party, but I don't know anybody that could get me in."

"You know me. We can go to the party together and eat afterwards."

She grabbed his face and kissed him on the lips and said, "Thank you so much for inviting me. It'll be a blast—you'll see."

"Probably so," he said hesitantly.

They walked back inside of the dealership and continued their conversation., but it was more on the level of catching up with each other because they hadn't seen each other since Greg and Jennifer had been on the outs of their relationship.

"Where do you work now?" he asked.

"I'm a paralegal at a firm near the Georgia Dome," she answered. "Once I finish grad school, I'm onto bigger and better things."

"What's your master's degree going to be in?"

"I will have my MBA at the end of December."

"That's what's up. So, working as a paralegal is a means to an end, huh?"

"Yeah, and I have to stay focused."

"And you will."

"What about you? When are you taking the CPA exam again?"

"I'm taking the exam again on Tuesday. Wish me luck."

"You don't need luck. I'll say a prayer for you, and you'll do fine."

"Thanks, I need all the help I can get."

"You're welcome."

"So, what time are you going to pick me up?" she asked, changing the subject.

"The party starts at nine, so I was planning on stopping through around ten. Then we can grab something to eat afterwards," he answered.

"That sounds great, but why don't we eat first? If the party is jumping like I think it's gonna be, it'll be too late to eat once it's over."

"You're right, so maybe I could pick you up around seven, okay?"

"Okay, that's fine."

They continued their conversation for another fifteen minutes before Pamela's car was ready. One of the technicians inform her that nothing was wrong with her vehicle, and that there was no charge. The rattling noise was a piece of debris stuck in between the rim and brake.

"I'll see you later on," she said.

"Looking forward to it," he said. "See you later."

"Bye, sweetie."

8

Rosalyn had been wandering aimlessly around Clark's campus after learning about Ramona's illness. She saw a few old friends and said hello to them, but she kept small talk to a bare minimum as she was in no shape to talk to anyone for long. She finally reached her car after thirty minutes of hobnobbing with old acquaintances and drove off. Call Jessica, she said as she put her earphones in.

"Hey, girl," Jessica said.

"Can you meet me somewhere to talk?" Rosalyn asked.

"Sure. Where do you want to meet?"

"I'm near campus, and I just saw Ramona. I can come by your place if you're home."

"Yeah, sure, come on by. I'm trying to pick out an outfit for tonight."

"The party...damn, I almost forgot."

"You forgot? I need you to be on point, Roz. This is only the biggest bash of the year."

"Don't worry, I'll bring my A game as always."

"You'd better. Hey, is everything okay?"

"I'll tell you about it when I get there."

"All right, see you in a few."

Rosalyn disconnected the call and headed to Jessica's. She wiped away some tears as she reminisced about the first time she met Ramona and Sasha at freshman orientation. Ramona and Sasha were giggling and looking in her direction, and she had taken offense to that.

"Is something funny?" Rosalyn asked, directing her question at Ramona. "Because I'm giving out two-for-one specials on beat-downs."

"Relax, girl," Ramona said. "You're rockin' the hell out of that dress, though."

"Huh?" Rosalyn asked. "What are you saying?"

"A dress and stilettos?" Sasha asked. "This is freshman orientation, not happy hour after work."

41

"Don't hate," Rosalyn said. "This is who I am…you have to dress for success."

"You don't have any casual wear?" Sasha asked. "You know you can rock some skinny jeans and still look fly."

"No, I don't have any casual wear," Rosalyn answered. "Everybody in the hood dresses like that…I want to be different."

"Where are you from?" Ramona asked.

"Chicago," Rosalyn answered.

"Well, Chi-town," Sasha said, "we're about to go to the mall, and you should roll with us."

"I'm supposed to meet my boyfriend after I register for classes," Rosalyn said.

"You can see him later," Ramona urged. "Come on, let's go."

"Well, okay," Rosalyn said.

"Is that your real hair color?" Sasha asked. "I've never seen hair that red on a black girl before."

"You are black, aren't you?" Ramona asked.

"My mother is white and my father is black, so what does that make me?" Rosalyn asked rhetorically.

"Confused," Sasha joked.

"Don't pay her any attention," Ramona added.

"What-ever," Rosalyn said.

"What's your name, Chi-town?" Sasha asked.

"Rosalyn," she replied.

"I'm Sasha, and this is my cousin Ramona," Sasha said.

"Nice to meet both of you," Rosalyn said.

"Likewise," Ramona said.

"Where are you all from?" Rosalyn asked.

"Fayetteville, North Carolina," Sasha answered.

"I love your accent, Sasha," Rosalyn said. "You sound like a real southern belle."

"Thank you," Sasha said. "I couldn't tell where you're from though—you talk so proper."

"My mother made me read one book a week until I turned eighteen," Rosalyn said. "She teaches high school English."

"Damn, girl, that's rough," Ramona said. "You hang around us long enough, we'll have you dressing hood and talking street slang in no time."

"Don't pay her any mind," Sasha said. "She got dropped on her head as a baby."

"Are you trying to call me slow?" Ramona asked.

"If the shoe fits…"

"Girl, shut up."

"No, Ramona, you shut up."

Rosalyn laughed to herself as she wiped away the rest of her tears, and she parked her car in front of Jessica's apartment complex. Jessica buzzed her in once she rang her bell.

"What's up, Jessie?" Rosalyn asked as she gave Jessica a hug.

"Nothing much," Jessica replied. "You look like you lost your best friend."

"Ramona has stage four cancer."

"Oh, no! How is that even possible?"

"I know…she's way too young to die. What am I going to do without her?"

"I'm so sorry, Roz. Ramona is such a good person."

"The best…"

"Come here."

Jessica embraced Rosalyn for a moment after she started crying. Jessica then got a box of Kleenex off of the living room table.

"Here," Jessica said as she handed Rosalyn the Kleenex.

"Thank you," Rosalyn said.

"Does Sasha know about this?"

"No, and Mona swore me to secrecy because she wants to be the one who tells her."

"I'm glad you told me…you know you can confide in me anytime you need to."

"Thanks, I appreciate that."

"So, is she receiving treatment?"

"Not anymore—she said there's nothing the doctors can do for her because the cancer has spread."

"I feel so sorry for Ramona. Shame on her to make you keep something like that in, though."

"Don't blame her—she's a very private person."

"I don't—can't imagine what she's going through."

Rosalyn noticed Greg's leather jacket on the sofa and asked, "Is that Greg's jacket on the couch?"

"Yeah, he's going to be staying with me for a while," Jessica replied. "Greg and Jennifer broke up."

"Why?"

"She's cheating on him, and I'm so damn pissed about it."

"That's so messed up. I feel bad for him."

"He's okay…at least he seems to be okay. You should give him a call before he's off the market."

"Maybe I will. This might just be my chance to get him back."

"You two would be good together. I love the person you've become, Roz. There's nobody better suited for him than you because you understand him better than anyone else does."

"Thanks. That means a lot to me."

"It's the truth, girl. I'm tired of seeing these women try to take advantage of him. I really hope it works out for you two this time."

"Me, too. I'll give it my best shot."

"You know," Jessica said, pausing for a second, "I really thought Jennifer was a down-to-Earth type of chick, but she had me totally fooled."

"I'm going to be totally honest with you, Jessie," Rosalyn said. "I never really bought into Greg being with her because I always felt that she was a rebound. Even though it seemed like he'd moved on, I knew it wouldn't last."

"She's as fake as a three-dollar bill is what she is."

"That was your girl, Jessie. I never liked her."

"So, what time do you wanna head over to the club?" Jessica asked.

"We should get there around six, I think," Rosalyn answered.

"Yeah, that'll give us plenty of time to get prepared."

"Is Greg coming?"

"He said he was."

"Good. Let the games begin."

9

Pamela checked herself in the full-length mirror hanging on the bathroom door. She tried on a sheer black outfit that looked like a short blouse that buttoned down to her navel in the front and a dress that draped to her calves in the back, and she accessorized this blouse with a black tube top and matching hip-hugging shorts that accentuated her voluptuous thighs and derriere.

"I look good," she said to herself. "Greg won't know what hit him when he sees me in this."

She continued to look at herself in the mirror for a few minutes more and made sure everything was satisfactory. She then put on her four-inch stilettos, her gold hoop earrings, her necklace and bracelet that complimented her earrings perfectly, and she was ready in record time before Greg arrived for their date. She had about an hour to kill, so she decided to give her soro Tameka a call.

"Hey, Pam," Tameka said. "How you been?"

"I'm good, girl," Pamela said. "You'll never guess who I'm going on a date with."

"Who?"

"Come on, guess?"

"I don't know...you're going on a date with a professional athlete."

"Nope."

"Who?"

"I have a date with Greg."

"Greg? How the hell do you have a date with Greg when you know he's with Jennifer?"

"He broke up with Jennifer yesterday."

"Damn, Pam, you didn't waste any time, did you?"

"It's not even like that..."

"Then what is it like? The sheets on their bed aren't even cold yet, and you're trying to push up on Greg like some thirsty trick."

"Girl, please...Greg ain't your man."

"Whatever, Pam. So, why did they break up?"

"Jennifer was cheating on him."

"Damn, that's crazy. She cut me off for merely flirting with Greg at Sasha and Horace's engagement party, and now she's sleeping with somebody else behind his back. She's got some nerve."

"Yeah, and she tried to justify herself to me this morning."

"Does she know you're going out with her man?"

"Ex-man, Meka, and no, she doesn't know. I don't rock with her anymore."

"Well, that makes two of us."

"Are you mad at me?"

"Girl, no...do your thing. You're my sister, and that's never going to change."

"That's good to know, Meka. I already lost Jennifer as a friend...I don't want to lose you, too."

"That's not gonna happen. If you're down with me, I'm down with you."

"Good. I'll let you know how my date with Greg goes."

"You do that. Talk to you later."

"Okay, bye."

Pamela disconnected the call and sat on the sofa in deep thought afterwards. Tameka's words and tone rang in her head, and she couldn't shake the feeling she was having. People say one thing and do another every day of the week, and she wondered what Tameka really thought about her dating Greg. Tameka could be really messy when provoked, and even though they were good friends, the memory of what she did to Jennifer was still fresh in her mind.

She turned on the television to get her mind off of Tameka and continued to wait for Greg. He was a catch in her mind, and she was willing to sacrifice her friendship with Tameka to get him.

10

Greg stuffed the trunk of his car with his last box full of accounting and business books and closed it shut. His back seat obstructed his rear view with several large plastic storage containers full of clothes and shoes, and his flat screen television sat securely on the floor on one side and a box of CDs and DVDs on the other side. He reserved a small storage unit not far from Jessica's apartment, and he sat his suitcase with the clothes he was going to wear for duration of his stay with her on the front seat. He didn't take any of the furniture that they had in the apartment, so there was no need to rent a U-Haul.

He went back inside and left the key on the living room table. He then locked the door behind him and dashed back to his car.

"Call Horace," he instructed Siri, while he leaned against the driver side door of his car with his phone to his ear.

"What's up, my dude?" Horace asked.

"Nothing much," Greg answered. "I'm going to Jessie's promotion party tonight."

"What?"

"I know…me going to a party, right?"

"Go have some fun, man. I wish I were there with you."

"Yeah, me too."

"Is Jennifer going with you?"

"Jen and I broke up…"

"No way, man…I don't believe it."

"Believe it, my brother. She was cheating on me with her boss. I just finished packing my stuff and bounced."

"Unbelievable. I thought she had more class than that."

"She dissed me, bruh—she basically called me a nobody because I work at McDonald's."

"You don't need her, Greg. If she can't see that your situation is temporary or a means to an end, then she's blind. And she will be a liability to you in the long-run."

"You're right. She's a great actress, you know, because I didn't see any of this coming, but I'm done trying to figure her out."

"Now I feel kind of guilty because I was the one who encouraged you to push up on her in the first place."

"Are you kidding me? This isn't your fault. I saw a pot of honey and licked it clean, and I'm totally responsible for my own actions."

"I'm sorry, Greg. I wish it was something I could do for you."

"I'm straight, man. I'm gonna stay with Jessie for a while."

"That's good. If you need anything at all, I'm here for you."

"Thanks."

"Anything for my brother."

"Enough about that, though. I can't wait to cut up with you next week."

"Yeah, the bachelor party is going to be mad crazy, but the party is for you all. I'm going be on my best behavior."

"I totally understand that. It's tradition though, and who are we to break tradition?"

"We can't get too out of hand because breakfast starts at nine at my dad's house in the Hamptons. We have a full plate of activities all the way up to the wedding on Sunday."

"Damn, Horace, you come from a world that I don't have a clue about…I mean, breakfast in the Hamptons? Man that sounds really crazy to me."

"We're just regular people with a lot of money, that's all."

"I can't even relate because I've been broke my whole life."

"Don't let any of that fool you…my family has problems just like any other family."

"Like your parents splitting up."

"Exactly."

Horace paused and said, "I envy you flying solo to the party because I've always wanted to kick it at a soiree like that. I know it's going be some celebrities there."

"I'm not exactly flying solo…"

"Who are you kickin' it with?"

"Jen's friend Pam."

"Hell no, man! You're being really sloppy."

"Come on, man, it's not even like that. She really wanted to go to the party, so I invited her."

"Watch it, Greg. Pam seems cool and all, but don't get caught up. What kind of woman would push up on her best friend's man anyway?"

"Believe me, I thought about that, too. Don't worry, I'm not going to do anything stupid."

"All I'm saying is be careful. I don't trust people who are willing to cross that line no matter what the circumstances may be. Jennifer cheating on you doesn't have anything to do with her."

"I know, and you're right."

Greg paused and said, "I am a little psyched about hanging out in Buckhead. I've never been on that side of town since I've been in Atlanta."

"That's what's up."

There was momentary silence, and then Greg asked, "Are you sure you're ready to tie the knot?"

"Yes, I'm ready. I knew I wanted to spend the rest of my life with her the moment she took me back."

"How did you know? I mean, what was the one thing about Sasha that made you propose to her?"

"The first time Sasha cooked for me, I knew that she could potentially be the one. She did stuff for me that a wife would do from day one of me dating her."

"That's dope. I certainly appreciated her when we were roommates."

"The same type of woman is out there waiting for you too, Greg. Sometimes that very thing that we're looking for is right in front of us."

"Oh, yeah? And what is that supposed to mean?"

"Sasha asked me how you and Jennifer were doing, and I told her that you all were having problems. Then she brought up Rosalyn, and I said you weren't going down that road again. Is that still true?"

"Yeah, I'm never going back to her, Horace. What she did rocked me to my core, man. I mean…I'm not even the same person that I was because of her leaving me the way she did, and I don't think I ever will be."

"I hear what you're saying, but she really has changed, bro. It might not be a bad idea if you gave her another shot…I'm just saying."

"You may be right, but the truth is I don't feel the same way about her anymore. I got love for her because we grew up together, but I love her like I love my sister Jessica."

"I totally understand, bro."

"Well, I'm on my way to pick up Pam. I'll see you next week."

"Okay, enjoy yourself, man. You deserve to have some fun."

"Thanks…talk to you later."

"Peace, Greg."

11

Sasha arrived in Atlanta inside of the six o'clock hour and immediately tried to call Ramona, but got no answer. After she retrieved her luggage in baggage claim at Hartsfield-Jackson Airport, she then logged into the Uber app on her phone and requested a ride. There was an available driver already parked in the ride-sharing area of the airport with his hazard lights on, and she noticed that his car was dirty and frowned.

She then opened the rear door on the right side and tossed her bag on the seat before she got in. I'm going to deduct a point on this driver's Uber rating for having me in a dirty car, she thought. He'd better get me to Ramona's house in record time.

"Hello, Sasha, welcome to Atlanta," he said.

"Hi," Sasha said.

"Is this your first time visiting Atlanta?" he asked.

"No, it isn't," Sasha answered curtly.

"Oh, okay."

He could sense that Sasha didn't want to talk and remained silent for the duration of the ride. Fortunately, traffic was light, and they arrived at Ramona's in about twenty minutes.

"Enjoy your stay in Atlanta," he said. "Take care."

"Thank you," Sasha said. Her mood seemed to lighten somewhat.

She grabbed her bag and hopped out of the back seat before shutting the door. She rang Ramona's bell a minute later but got no response. Luckily, she still had an extra key to her place. When she finally got to Ramona's apartment and opened the front door, everything looked exactly like she remembered it. She certainly wasn't the interior decorator that Sasha was and made no qualms about it.

"Ramona!" she shouted. "It's Sasha."

She scanned the living room and kitchen and proceeded to check the bedroom once she saw that the bathroom was also unoccupied.

She saw Ramona in her bed with her eyes closed once she entered the room.

"Ramona," she said as she shook her. "Wake up, Ramona."

"Huh," Ramona said, still groggy from her deep sleep. "What are you doing here, Sasha?"

"You're not answering any of my calls, so I came down here to check on you," Sasha answered. "You didn't hear me calling you just now?"

"No," Ramona answered. "I took these painkillers once Roz left—turned off the ringer of my phone and have been asleep ever since."

"Roz was just here?"

"Yeah, she was here early this afternoon."

"What's going on with you, Ramona? I haven't talked to you in months, and my wedding is next week."

"I'm dying, Sasha…"

"Dying? Girl, quit playing."

"I have stage four cervical cancer, and there's nothing else the doctors can do for me. I haven't had the strength to do anything these last few weeks."

Tears began to flow freely from Sasha's eyes, and she asked, "Why didn't you tell me?"

"I couldn't find the right words to tell you," Ramona answered. "I still can't even wrap my own mind around it."

Sasha sat next to Ramona on her bed and buried her face in her hands. She was wailing uncontrollably at that point, and Ramona put her arm around her and kissed her on the cheek in an attempt to soothe her pain.

"What am I going to do without you?" Sasha asked. "You've been with me my whole life, and now you're going to leave me?"

"I'm sorry, Sasha," Ramona said. "I don't want to die, but I'm in so much pain."

"There has to be something that we can do. I'm not ready to let you go."

"Unfortunately, it's not up to us. I don't want to let you go, either, but we have to prepare for the worst."

"I'm not trying to hear that right now! Stop saying that!"

"It's the truth, Sasha. We can tell Momma together."

"I'm postponing the wedding…"

"No, you can't do that. You and Horace have worked too hard to plan this wedding, and I'm not going to let you cancel it on my account."

Ramona tried to stand up but stumbled onto the floor. She started coughing uncontrollably as Sasha tried to help her to her feet, and some blood trickled from her mouth and dripped to the floor.

"Come on, I'm taking you to the hospital," Sasha said. "Let's get you dressed."

"No, I don't want to go to the hospital," Ramona said. "I don't want to die in a damn hospital."

"You're not dying today," Sasha said. "Come on, let's get you dressed, I said."

Sasha went to the bathroom to get a washcloth so that she could wipe the blood from Ramona's mouth. Ramona sat on her bed and tried to disrobe herself, but she couldn't muster up the strength to undress. Sasha entered the bedroom with a damp washcloth and sat next to Ramona on the bed. She wiped Ramona's mouth and asked, "How do you feel?"

"Not good, Sasha," Ramona replied. "My entire body aches, and I feel dizzy."

"I'm going to call 911."

Ramona didn't protest, and Sasha made the call. She slowly helped Ramona get dressed and had her ready right before the ambulance arrived. The paramedics then asked a series of questions before placing Ramona on the gurney, and Sasha accompanied them to the hospital by riding in the front seat of the ambulance.

Sasha connected her earphones to her phone before placing them in her ears and called Horace.

"Hey, baby, what's up?" Horace asked.

"It's not good, honey," she answered.

"What's wrong?"

"Ramona's very sick. She has cancer, and I don't know how long I'm going to be out here."

"Cancer? Is she going to be okay?"

"No, I don't think so, Horace. She's stage four, and the doctors don't give her much time to live."

"I'm very sorry, sweetheart. I'm going to catch the next plane down there."

"Okay, call me when you land. We'll be at Grady Memorial Hospital."

"Okay, and I'll pray for Ramona."

"Thank you, baby. I really need you right now."

"You're welcome. I love you, Sasha, and I'll see you soon."

"I love you, too."

12

Greg arrived at Pamela's place a few minutes before seven o'clock. He didn't want to be too early because he thought it would make him seem too anxious, and he didn't want to be late because he thought it would give the impression that he didn't care. He motioned to get out of his car, but Pamela was in the window and stepped out of her apartment complex seconds later. He got out anyway and opened the passenger side door for her, and he was literally blown away when he saw her outfit.

He stretched out his arms for a hug and said, "Damn, Pam, you look amazing."

"Thank you, Greg," she said after giving him a warm embrace and a kiss on the cheek. "You look pretty dapper yourself."

"Thank you. So, are you hungry?"

"I can definitely eat."

"You like Chinese food? Because I got us a reservation at Hsu's."

"I love Chinese food, and Hsu's is great."

"Good, let's go."

They left, and there was silence for the first few seconds of the ride to the restaurant on Peachtree Center Avenue in downtown Atlanta. Pamela quickly broke the ice and said, "So, have you talked to Jennifer today?"

"Unfortunately, yes," Greg answered. "She called me earlier and asked me when I was going to move my stuff out of the apartment."

"Wow, she's kicking you out already."

"It's cool…I needed closure, and this is one step closer in that direction."

Pamela took a deep breath and said, "I really like you, Greg. I know that you want to take things slow, and I respect that. However, just know that I want to earn your trust, and I would never hurt you."

"I'm very flattered, but I'm a big boy. My heart isn't made of glass, and besides, getting hurt is a part of life."

"I know you're a big boy, Greg. I just want you to know how I feel."

"And I really like you, too, Pam. Any guy would be lucky to have you."

"And I'm yours if you want me, baby. Let me mend your broken heart."

"Hold up—is that how you see me? Broken? Weak?"

"No, I didn't mean it like that. It wasn't my intention to upset you..."

"Nah, it's cool, Pam, and I'm not upset. It's just that I don't want you or anybody else viewing me as broken, fragile, or weak, because I'm none of those things."

"You're right, and I'm sorry you took what I said the wrong way. What I meant to say is you're a strong and successful man who's fine as hell."

"Thank you, that's very kind of you to say."

"So, Greg, what do you really think of me?"

"Well, for starters, I think you're very classy and sexy, and you're a woman who knows what she wants and knows how to go after it. I also see that you're high-maintenance and like the finer things."

"High-maintenance? You think I'm stuck up?"

"No, I don't think you're stuck up. I just paid you at least three compliments, and all you thought was 'stuck up'?"

"I'm just saying..."

"There's nothing wrong with a woman being high-maintenance, Pam. You're on your way to receiving your master's degree and possibly running your own business someday, and I'm on my way to passing the CPA exam and becoming an accountant. We both desire the finer things in life and are willing to work for them."

"I see your point. I guess that makes you high-maintenance, too."

"Guys can't be high-maintenance."

"I beg to differ...my ex stayed in the mirror almost as much as I did."

They arrived at Hsu's, and Greg parked in the garage above Hsu's. They stepped inside of the restaurant, and the hostess looked up their reservation before seating them. Water and silverware were already placed on their table, and the server gave them their menus. Greg sat next to Pamela instead of sitting across from her.

"Your server will be with you shortly," the hostess said.

"Thank you," Greg said.

Pamela took a sip of her water and asked, "Well then, why did you step to Jennifer instead of me?"

"Because I thought you still had something going on with Brian, and I wasn't aware of the fact that you were even interested in me," Greg answered.

"For the record, Brian and I were done, and I've been interested in you since the first time we met."

"Well, I never got that vibe from you—I would've asked you out if I'd known you were interested."

"So, you were interested in me, too?"

"Yes, I was. A blind man could clearly see that you're a catch."

Pamela grabbed Greg's hand before looking into his eyes and said, "I think we should make up for lost time."

Greg locked in on her alluring gaze and said, "Maybe we should."

Greg then paused and said, "Brian did make it seem as though you two still hooked up from time to time."

"Brian's a liar," Pamela said abruptly. "And I haven't been intimate with anyone since we broke up. I've been on a few dates, but that's it."

"My bad...I didn't know."

"You don't have to apologize. He's a jerk."

"Why did you all break up?" Greg asked. "You two seemed like the perfect couple."

"Things were good in the beginning, but I realized later on that we wanted different things out of life," Pamela answered solemnly.

"Different things..."

"He wanted me to take care of the home and raise our children while he made the money, but that's not what I wanted."

"What did you want?"

"To be a successful career as a businesswoman, for starters."

"Do you ever want to get married? Have kids?"

"Someday."

"I understand. You want to establish your career first—then have a family."

"That's the idea. I didn't go to college to be a stay-at-home mom."

"I sympathize with you."

The server walked over to their table and said, "My name is Jia, and I will be your server tonight. Can I get you something to drink?"

"I want a Pepsi or Coke," Pamela said.

"Is Coke okay?" Jia asked.

"Yes, that's fine," Pamela answered.

"And you, sir?" Jia asked.

"I'll have the same," Greg answered.

"Are you ready to order?" Jia asked.

"Yes," Pamela answered. "I'll have the sea scallops in black pepper sauce."

"And you, sir?" Jia asked.

"Let me have the curry chicken," Greg answered.

"I'll put that in for you," Jia said, before walking back to the kitchen.

"So, what about you?" Pamela asked.

"Huh?" Greg asked.

"What do you want out of life, Greg?"

"I thought I had everything that I could possibly want—a beautiful woman who adored me, and I was working my way up to becoming a successful accountant. I was really happy, Pam, or so I thought, but Jennifer totally blindsided me. Now, I don't know what I want."

"I'm truly sorry about that. My girl really did a number on you."

"All she had to do was come to me. If she wasn't happy with the situation, she should've just broken up with me instead."

"Maybe she didn't want to hurt you."

"That's no excuse. A guy is labeled a dog for cheating, but when a woman does it, there's always a reason why she did it."

"I know, and you're right, baby. I'm a straight shooter, and if I'm not happy about something, you'll be the first to know about it."

"That's good to know."

"I wasn't going to tell you this, but you really hurt my feelings awhile back."

"How did I hurt your feelings, Pam?"

"It was the night my sorority threw our annual end-of-the-year bash junior year, and you took my hand and led me to the dance floor. I really felt something for you that night and thought you felt the same way, but I found out later you hooked up with Jen…"

"I didn't mean to give you the wrong impression. It was also the same night I saw Rosalyn and Dave together for the first time, and I wasn't in the right frame of mind after that. Jennifer was there for me when I was in a lot of pain. I'm sorry, Pam."

"Don't be. I knew you only danced with me to make Rosalyn jealous, and I'm not even mad at you for that."

"I couldn't let her know that she had gotten to me, and you were my only lifeline. Otherwise, I might have snapped off and caused a scene."

"Rosalyn and Jennifer are your past, and I want to be your future, Greg. You're a good man who has a lot to offer a woman, and I promise your heart is safe with me."

She turned toward him and tasted his lips for the second time that day. This particular kiss was everything that she'd imagined and more, but she reluctantly pulled herself away from him seconds later.

"Did I do something wrong?" a puzzled Greg asked.

"No, sweetheart," Pamela answered. "It's not you, it's me."

"What?"

"I don't want to fall in love with you too fast, and if I keep this up, that's exactly what's going to happen."

"Maybe I want you to fall in love with me because I'm starting to feel the same way about you."

They then indulged themselves in French kissing each other briefly before regaining their composure. She subsequently intertwined her fingers with his and said, "I'm really feelin' you, and I hope to see more of you in the future."

"I'd like that very much."

Jia had brought their food minutes later, and they continued to converse and enjoy each other's company. An hour more had past, and Greg was ready for the bill once they finished dinner.

"We don't have to go to party," Pamela suggested. "We can go back to my place for a nightcap."

"As tempting as that sounds, we can't do that right now," Greg said. "I promised Jessie I'd come to the party, and that's what we're gonna do."

"Okay, that's fine, but you're spending the night with me when we're done partying."

"I'm not ready for that yet, either, Pam. I still want to take things slow."

"I'm sorry, Greg...I didn't mean to get ahead of myself."

They left Hsu's, and they began kissing each other again in the parking garage while standing next to Greg's car. Pamela somehow managed to get Greg to let his guard down completely by skillfully tapping into the reptilian part of his brain. She stroked his ego to the point that it rendered him virtually helpless in her presence, and he was ready to break all of his rules because of it.

They continued their groping session inside of the car, and she unzipped his pants after massaging his endowment. He removed her hand from his groin and said, "Not like this...this isn't how I get down."

"Me, neither," she said. "I don't know what came over me...I hope you don't think any less of me."

"No, Pam, I don't. I want us to start our relationship the right way, not revel in some cheap thrill in the parking lot."

"Are we in a relationship, Greg?"

"Yes, I feel that things are blossoming into one."

"Yes, baby, it's definitely blossoming into something special."

"I also want you to know that I'm not a dog who'll get busy with any random chick in a public place."

"I know you're not a dog," she said before pecking him on the lips. "Otherwise, I wouldn't be checking for you, boo."

"One more thing…"

"What is it, baby?"

"I want us to be celibate until I know you're the right woman for me and I'm the right man for you. I'm starting to believe that premarital sex is the downfall of most relationships, and I don't want us to be doomed before we even get started."

"I'm going to be completely honest with you, Greg. I've been celibate since I broke up with Brian, and I made a promise to myself that I would marry the next guy that I'm intimate with."

"So, would you be able to wait until we know that we're meant to be together?"

"Yes, baby, I think you're worth the wait."

"Good. Let's go before Jessie sends out a search party for me."

13

Marcus had finally gotten hold of Jennifer and convinced her to meet him at their favorite hotel in downtown Atlanta. They were supposed to meet at the Fairfield Inn on Peachtree Street to discuss the status of their relationship. Marcus was parked in the lot facing the entrance and was waiting on Jennifer to show up. He looked at his watch, which read 8:52 p.m., and started fidgeting. Ten additional minutes passed before Jennifer's black BMW slowly entered the parking lot. Marcus then got out of his car and motioned over to her car.

"What took you so long?" he asked.

"I had stuff to do, Marcus," she answered.

"What stuff?"

"Let's not go there."

"I asked you a question, Jennifer."

"I'm not all in your business when you have to do *family* stuff with your wife."

"That's not fair. You're still messing around with Greg, aren't you?"

"What? I told you we broke up."

"Then are you seeing somebody else?"

"This jealousy thing is so unbecoming of you, Marcus. Why did you drag me out here anyway?"

"I want us to be together, Jennifer. I can't live without you."

"Prove it...I'm not wasting anymore time with you or this relationship that appears to be going nowhere."

"I left her, Jennifer. I told my wife everything, and I packed my bags and left."

"You told your wife about us?"

"Yes, that's what I've been trying to tell you...I told her the truth, and she kicked me out the house."

"I've been waiting for you to tell me this for so long! I love you so much, Marcus!"

"I love you, too!"

She pulled him close to her and began kissing him passionately. He released his embrace and said, "Let's go to my room and finished what we just started."

"You're staying here?"

"Yes, ever since last night."

"Not anymore. You're moving in with me."

"What about Greg?"

"He moved all of his things out today."

"Come on, baby. Let's go inside."

They quickly entered the hotel and went to the twelfth floor. They undressed in record time and were completely indulging themselves in each other's sinful treats.

"I want to make love to you," she said. "I'm going to give this to you every night."

"Yes, baby, please do," he shrieked. "This feels so damn good."

They intensely gazed into each other's eyes after their evening romp. He caressed her cheek and said, "I want to make love to you like this every night."

"And you can have me every night now that you're not with your wife anymore."

"So, what do we do now?" he asked, suddenly raising himself up from the bed.

"We live happily ever after, Marcus," she replied.

"It's not that simple."

"It is for me. You move in with me, you get a divorce, and we live happily ever after. End of story."

"Stacy is going to take me for everything I've got, Jennifer. I never got her to sign a prenup."

"Everything will work itself out, so relax."

"I cheated on her. No judge in the state of Georgia is going to rule in my favor."

"You're a multi-millionaire, Marcus. You can afford it."

"My kids…she's going to take my kids from me."

"No, she's not, Marcus. Give her time to calm down, and you'll work through it, baby. I'll be here for you every step of the way."

"Thank you, Jennifer. You're the best thing that has ever happened to me. I was so unhappy with Stacy, but you're the apple of my eye."

"You're welcome. I love you."

"I love you, too."

"Pack your things so that we can get out of here," she said as she put her panties and bra on.

"I have a confession to make."

"What is it, sweetheart?"

"I'm not a multi-millionaire…exactly."

"What do you mean exactly?" she asked, standing up from the bed.

"I have two million in a joint savings account with Stacy, and I'm still making huge payments on my house, car notes, and credit card payments," he answered solemnly.

"You're been with the firm for twenty years, and all you have in savings is two million? With the salary you make?"

"What do you want me to say? My soon-to-be-ex-wife has expensive taste. Hell, I was lucky to even save that much."

"What about stocks? Bonds?"

"The stock market crash wiped out most of what I had, so I panicked and put the rest in money market and mutual funds accounts."

"Well, you won't have that once your soon-to-be-ex-wife takes the rest of your money. You're be paying alimony from now to eternity and child support until your newborn finishes college."

"Come on. Help me pack my stuff so that we can go to your place."

"I don't know about this, Marcus. I need time to sort things out."

"Sort things out? I put my life on the line for you, and all you can say is you need to sort things out?"

"Yes, Marcus, I do. I might as well have stayed with Greg if I'd known you were this deep in debt."

"So, what, it was all about the money, Jennifer? What about love? I thought you loved me."

"What the hell does love have to do with it? I can do bad all by myself."

"I can still take care of us, Jennifer…"

"You can't possibly afford the lifestyle that I want to live, and you definitely can't take care of me."

"You know what, Jennifer? You're nothing but a gold-digging tramp!"

"And you're a damn liar!"

"Liar?! I never lied to you!"

"You led me to believe that you were in such great shape financially…the fancy restaurants, the exotic weekend vacations, and the three-hundred-thousand-dollar Bentley…"

"I, unlike you, can definitely afford the lifestyle that I live."

"Not if your wife takes half of your money. Have a nice life, Marcus. I'm out."

"You're not going anywhere, Jennifer!" he shouted as he grabbed her arm.

"Let me go, Marcus!" she shouted back, snatching her arm from his grasp. "You can go back to your wife because I don't want you anymore!"

"You can't just toss me aside like a pair of dirty underwear, dammit!"

"Watch me!"

"You can kiss your partnership and your job goodbye!"

"Yeah, and I'll sue you for sexual harassment and leave you broke, jobless, and homeless, loser!"

Jennifer finished getting dressed and stormed out of his hotel room. She marched down the hall toward the elevators and heard his footsteps behind her moments later, so she hastened her pace. She pushed the button, the elevator chimed, and the light above the door lit up before the door opened. She then quickly stepped inside and pushed the button to close the door seconds before Marcus could stick his arm inside to stop the elevator from going down.

Once she got to her car, she sighed and took her vial out of her purse. She then poured some coke on her index finger and snorted the porcelain-looking powder before recklessly exiting the parking lot.

14

They could see from a block away that the club was already packed, and the line was halfway down the block when Greg parked his car in the lot adjacent to the club. He looked at his watch, and it read nine forty-seven. He then got out of the car and opened the door for Pamela. He grabbed her hand, and they walked toward the back of the line.

"I know we're not about to stand in this long line," Pamela said.

"I don't think we have much of a choice, Pam," Greg said.

"The hell we don't," she said. "Greg, recognize who you are— your sister Jessica is the hottest radio personality in Atlanta. Need I say more?"

"Yo, do you see that guy at the door? I can tell he's gonna be a problem. I don't even feel like dealing with that madness."

"Come on, baby, you can do this. You'll never know unless you try...all that he can say is no."

"Okay, since you put it that way. Come on, let's do it."

They bypassed the line and approached the guy at the front entrance. He was a massive six-foot-four, three-hundred-pound bodybuilder with a Mohawk fade and tatted-up biceps. He smirked and motioned them to move out the way.

"Come on, man," Greg said, "give us a break."

"Why should I give you a break, man?" the guy asked. "Your girl is fine, though...she can get in."

"Sorry, sir, but we're a package deal," Pamela interjected. "I'm not going in without him."

"Suit yourself, gorgeous," he said. "It's invitation-only or ballers with deep pockets tonight. Sorry, my man."

"I was invited by Jessica O'Brien," Greg said. "She's my sister."

"Yeah, right," the bouncer said. "Jessica O'Brien from Power 108 is your sister?"

"Yeah, man, she is," Greg answered. "And I can prove it...here, take my ID."

The bouncer examined his driver's license and said, "So what, y'all have the same last name…that still doesn't prove anything. Get the hell outta here before I lose my temper."

"Man, the disrespect here is real," Greg said. "Come on, Pam, let's go."

"Sorry, baby," Pamela said, "he was such a jerk. You should call Jessica out here to handle this."

"Nah, that's okay. She's got enough going on right now."

Greg grabbed Pamela's hand, and they motioned toward the parking lot. Someone shouted out Greg's name before he could unlock his car door, and he quickly turned around and smiled.

"What's up, Greg?" the guy said. "You're leaving already?"

"I'm afraid so," Greg answered. "Homeboy won't let us in."

"Yeah?" he asked. "Don't even sweat that…I'll get you two in."

"Baby, this is Brandon Bostock of the Atlanta Hawks," Greg said.

"Nice to meet you," Brandon said, extending his hand to her. "All my friends call me Bebe."

"Likewise, Bebe," Pamela said as she shook his hand.

The three of them walked over to the front of the line, and Brandon nodded at the bouncer. The bouncer nodded back and said, "You know this dude, Bebe?"

"Yeah, Craig, Greg's a good friend of mine," Brandon answered. "We grew up together."

"Oh, yeah?" the bouncer asked.

"And he's Jessica's brother," Brandon added. "Give my man a break, Craig."

"Yeah, give us a break," Pamela said before she winked at Craig.

"My bad, y'all," Craig said, unhooking the purple velvet rope blocking the entrance. "Go on in."

"Thanks, I appreciate it," Greg said.

The three of them went inside and scanned the crowd as they walked by the bar. Brandon towered over nearly everyone at six foot ten, as he seemingly greeted half of the club. It was a packed house, and DJ Pandemonium was living up to his name by having the crowd jumping.

"What y'all drinking?" Brandon asked.

"I'll take a Grey Goose," Pamela replied.

"Miller Draft for me," Greg added.

"I'll be right back," Brandon said.

"You should tell Jessica what happened," Pamela said. "That guy didn't have to be so damn rude."

"Let it go, Pam," Greg said. "I have."

"That's what I love about you, Greg."

"What?"

"The way you let things roll off your back. You never seem to get too upset about anything. I wish I could be more like you."

"I like you the way you are. Don't change that for anyone."

"Thank you."

Brandon returned with the drinks moments later and said, "Your sister really knows how to throw a party, Greg," Brandon said. "I'm about to turn up."

"Thanks, bro," Greg said. "Next round's on me."

"Thank you," Pamela said.

"Don't worry about it, y'all," Brandon said. "Well, I'm single and about to mingle...enjoy the party."

"I will, and thanks for everything, Bebe," Greg said.

"Nice meeting you, Bebe," Pamela said.

Brandon ventured into the crowd, and Greg and Pamela continued to sip their drinks next to the bar. DJ Pandemonium rocked the house by blending a medley of a cappella rap songs with the classic instrumental version of "Burn" by Mobb Deep. They finished their drinks, and then Greg led Pamela to the dance floor. Greg felt a tap on the shoulder before they could really get into the music.

"Fancy seeing you two here," Jessica said.

Greg turned around, gave his sister a hug, and said, "This party is bumping, sis."

"I hope you didn't expect anything less," Jessica said. "Hi, Pam."

"Hey, girl," Pamela said.

"You're the only one of those Sigmas who isn't stuck up," Jessica said. "Your girl is gonna flip out when she finds out about you two."

"She isn't my girl anymore," Pamela said, "and what Greg and I do is none of her business."

"I heard that," Jessica said. "So, you two are an item now, Greg?"

"You can say that," Greg replied, putting his arm around Pamela's waist, "but we're going to take it slow."

"That's precious cargo you have there, Pam," Jessica said. "You be good to my brother, or else you and I are going to have a major problem."

"Don't worry, Jessica, Greg's in good hands," Pamela said.

"Well, enjoy the party," Jessica said. "I have to get back to work."

"Wait," Pamela said.

"What's up?" Jessica asked.

"One of your bouncers gave us a hard time at the door," Pamela answered.

"Let it go, Pam," Greg interjected.

"I can't let it go, baby," Pamela said.

"Which bouncer was it?" Jessica asked.

"His name is Craig," Pamela answered.

"Oh, okay," Jessica said. "Don't worry. I'll handle it."

Jessica walked away, and Greg and Pamela started dancing amidst the crowd of lively patrons. They couldn't feel the heat of Rosalyn's glare a few feet away, as she was standing near the entrance of the club and wasn't particularly enthusiastic about seeing them enjoying themselves. However, she decided to keep her distance and not cause a scene as she would have done in years past.

"Are you okay?" a young lady asked Rosalyn.

"Yes, I'm fine," Rosalyn answered.

"Is there anything else you need?"

"Check with Jessica and see if she's ready to start the raffle."

"Yes, boss, right away."

15

"What's your deal, Craig?" Jessica asked.

"I don't know what you're talking about," he answered.

"You turned my brother away."

"I didn't know that dude was your brother, Jessica."

"It shouldn't matter that he's my brother…everybody's welcome as long as they follow the dress code."

"It's already too many guys here…too many guys equals too many problems."

"The last time I checked, guys listen to our radio station, too. This isn't Ladies Night or about making the club hot…it's solely about the station gaining listeners and nothing else."

"I get it, Jessica, but let me do my job."

"Then do your job. I don't want to hear about any more issues tonight, understand?"

"Okay, I got it."

Jessica went back into the club, and Craig looked on in disgust as he continued to check people at the door. Rosalyn was at the DJ's table with a microphone in her hand. She had DJ Pandemonium cut the music so that she could address the crowd.

"May I have everyone's attention," Rosalyn said. "We're about to start the raffle, and we're going to give away three great prizes. Please pull out your drink tickets as I read off the numbers for third prize first."

Greg and Pamela examined their tickets as Rosalyn read off the six-digit number for third prize. Suddenly, someone in the crowd began shouting obscenities at another person.

"I said, get your hand out of my pocket!" a guy shouted.

Several bouncers rush over to the scrimmage and tried to defuse the situation, but one of the guys pulled out a gun. The other guy, who appeared to have beef with the patron brandishing the gun, pulled out his own gun.

"Back the hell up," Thug One said, pointing his gun directly at the four bouncers who bum-rushed him.

"You heard him," Thug Two said. "Put your hands up."

Jessica rushed over to the scene and said, "What's going on over here?"

"Back up, miss!" Thug Two said. "One false move, and I'm gonna stop your clock."

"All right, all right," Jessica said, "just don't point that gun at me."

Thug One put a mask on before marching over to the DJ's table, and he snatched the microphone from Rosalyn and said, "I want everybody's full cooperation or else!"

"Who do you think you are barging in here like this?" Rosalyn demanded.

Thug One pointed his gun in her face and shouted, "Move over there with the rest of the crowd before I put a bullet in your head!"

Rosalyn reluctantly walked over to the crowd of people standing in front of the DJ's table, and Thug One said, "Like I was saying before I was rudely interrupted, in case you all didn't know, this is a robbery. I demand everyone's full cooperation, or else I will kill anyone who doesn't get with the program."

Greg grabbed Pamela's hand and whispered, "Don't say anything. Let's just do exactly what they say and get through this alive."

"I'm so scared, Greg," she said.

"I know, but don't worry. I promise I won't let anything happen to you."

One of the male patrons tried to make a mad dash toward the exit, but a guy by the door pulled out a Glock and shot him in the chest. The crowd of people screamed in terror, and everyone remained still. Each one of the gang members revealed himself by putting on a black mask that covered the entire face except for the eyes and extracting a gun from his right boot, and they all aimed their guns directly at the crowd. There were twelve of them in total sprinkled throughout the club, and they ordered everyone to gather on the side away from the exit.

All of them were surprisingly well-dressed and had blended in with the crowd without arousing any type of suspicion prior to the ruckus. They ranged from five-foot-six to six-foot-three in height, and all had the same low-fade haircut.

The gang leader with the microphone shouted, "Everybody strip down to your underwear now! Anybody who doesn't comply will end up like that dead guy over there by the exit!"

"Hurry up!" one of the gang members amongst the crowd demanded. "And toss your phones, watches, jewelry, wallets, purses, and cash in one single pile!"

One of the young ladies said, "I don't have on any underwear."

"Me, either," another young lady said.

"I don't care," a second gang member said. "Take your damn clothes off now!"

Everybody took off their clothes and tossed their belongings in the pile as instructed, and a third gang member said, "Damn, these chicks are fine as hell. You, the naked girl with the big butt, come on over here so that I can sample the merchandise!"

"We don't have time for that," the gang member who shot and killed the patron said. "Stay where you are, miss."

"Why you trying to cock block, fam?"

"Are you trying to go back to prison, stupid? And if you mess up my money, I'm gonna shoot you, too."

"Enough!" the gang leader said. "Grab all the stuff so we can bounce, dammit!"

Sirens could be heard in the distance as the gang gathered all the cell phones, wallets, purses, cash and jewelry and tossed them in the laundry bags that they pulled out from their fanny packs. One of the gang members had been going through the pockets of the clothes on the floor when another one of them said, "Forget that…we gotta get the hell out of here!"

"One of them tipped the cops!" another one of them said. "Let's go!"

"It's been real, people," the leader said. "Thank you for your cooperation."

The treacherous twelve stormed out of the club and scurried to a van parked in front of the entrance. It sped off seconds later, as most of the crowd stood frozen in shock while trying to process what had just taken place. Greg put his arms around Pamela as she began sobbing on his shoulder. He released his embrace a few minutes later and gathered his slacks, his shirt, and Pamela's blouse and shorts. They slowly began to put their clothes on, and the rest of the crowd followed suit.

"My whole life was in that purse," Pamela said. "My phone, my debit and credit cards, and my driver's license. What am I going to do?"

"You can replace all of those things, Pam," Greg answered. "However, you can't replace your life."

"I know, but I can't help how I feel," Pamela said.

Jessica ran up to Greg and gave him a tight embrace. He looked toward the exit and noticed a guy checking the dead man's pulse. The guy shook his head at the small group of people standing around him.

"Are you okay?" Greg asked her.

"Yes, I am," Jessica answered.

"All right," Greg said.

"I thought I was going to die," Jessica said.

"I've never seen someone get murdered right in front of my face like that," Greg said.

"Me, either," Jessica said.

"I have," Pamela said as she put on her stilettos and wrapped her right arm around Greg's waist afterwards. "I saw a guy get shot in the head on my block in Chicago few years ago. It's no joke on the West Side."

"It's no joke in Englewood either," Greg added, "and that's why I'm never moving back to that neighborhood."

Rosalyn had joined the group of them moments later. Jessica gave her a warm embrace, and Greg followed suit with a hug and a kiss on Rosalyn's cheek.

"Are you okay, Roz?" Jessica asked.

"Yeah, I'll live," she answered. "How are you doing, Greg?"

"I'm okay," he answered. "This had been one hell of a night."

"No doubt about it," Rosalyn said. "I didn't expect to see you here, Pam. Are you and Greg a couple now?"

"Damn, you just get right to it, don't you, Rosalyn?" Pamela asked.

"I don't believe in beating around the bush," Rosalyn answered.

"Relax, ladies," Greg instructed. "Now is not the time or the place for this right now."

"I was just asking a question," Rosalyn said.

"Let it go, Roz," Jessica added.

The police and paramedics had finally arrived a few minutes later, and Rosalyn and Jessica accompanied by the bouncers walked toward the entrance to answer questions. Greg's phone rang, and he pulled it out of his pocket to answer it.

"Hello?" he asked.

"Hey, Greg," Sasha answered. "I've been trying to reach everybody, but you're the only one who picked up."

"Is everything all right?"

"No, Greg, I'm afraid not. I'm in Atlanta at Grady Memorial…"

"Grady Memorial? Are you hurt?"

"It's not me; it's my cousin Ramona. She's not going to make it through the night."

"What happened?"

"Just let Rosalyn and Jessica know what's going on and get over here as soon as you all can."

"Okay, we'll be there as soon as possible."

Greg ended the call, and Pamela asked, "Who was that?"

"That was Sasha," he answered. "She said Ramona's in the hospital, and that she probably won't make it through the night."

"Oh my God, what happened?"

"Don't know…she'll tell us when we get there."

"How do you still have your phone?"

"I still have my wallet and keys, too. I left everything but my watch in my pants pockets. Damn, that was my favorite watch…"

"Baby, you're something else."

"What? I wasn't going to make it easy for them. If they wanted my stuff, they were going to have to search my damn pockets for it."

16

"Did you notice anything out of the ordinary about any one of them?" the policeman asked. "Any scars or tattoos?"

"I didn't get a good look at any of their faces because they all put masks on after that guy got shot," Greg answered. "I can say that they were all well-groomed and very organized also for the most part—not your typical street gang."

"Okay," the policeman said.

"Each one of them drew their guns from the right boot," Jessica said. "And the leader was about six feet tall with a gold tooth."

"The right boot?" the policeman asked. "And the leader was six feet tall with a gold tooth?"

"Yes, and each gunman had on patent leather boots that came right above the ankle," Pamela added.

They continued to answer questions for another few minutes before Greg abruptly interrupted the officer. Rosalyn was silent and distant the entire interrogation.

"I hate to cut this short, officer," Greg said, "but a very dear friend of ours is lying in the hospital dying as we speak. We really need to get there as soon as possible."

"I'm sorry to hear about your friend, young man," the policeman said. "I think I have everything I need from you guys for now. Here, take my card and call me if you remember anything else, and I hope your friend pulls through."

"Thank you, officer," Greg said.

The policeman walked toward another group being questioned by a second officer, and Greg, Pamela, Rosalyn and Jessica rushed out the exit and hastened toward the parking lot.

"We can all ride together," Greg suggested.

"Okay," Jessica said. "I took an Uber anyway because I knew I'd be drinking later on."

"Rosalyn?" Greg asked. "They didn't take your stuff?"

"No, my purse was in one of the offices in the back of the club," she answered. "I'll meet you all there."

"All right," Greg said.

Rosalyn hit the alarm button of her car that was parked a couple of spaces away from Greg's car. She sped off before Greg could start his car and everybody got seated. Greg then rushed out the parking lot behind her and headed in the direction of Grady Memorial Hospital, which was about fifteen minutes away from the club.

"Roz isn't taking this too well," Jessica said. "She didn't say two words the whole time the police officer was questioning us."

"Ramona is her best friend," Greg said solemnly.

"I feel so bad for her," Pamela said.

"She cried uncontrollably once she found out Ramona had stage four cancer," Jessica said.

"What?" Greg asked, turning around to look Jessica in the eye at the stop light. "Cancer? She's too damn young to have stage four cancer."

"I'm afraid so," Jessica said.

"When did you find out about it?" Pamela asked.

"We both just found out about it today," Jessica answered. "Roz went by Ramona's apartment this afternoon to see her, and that's when Ramona told her the news. Roz was so devastated afterwards that she came by to see me."

"Damn, I can't get a green light to save my life," Greg said.

"Relax, Greg, and please get us there in one piece," Jessica said.

They arrived at the hospital thirteen minutes later, and the ambulance carrying the dead patron from the club arrived at the same time. Greg let everyone out at the emergency entrance.

"I'm going to find parking," Greg said. "I'll see you all in a few minutes."

"Okay, baby," Pamela said.

Greg spotted Rosalyn in the lot walking toward the emergency entrance while looking for an empty space. He quickly parked his car and hopped out.

"Rosalyn!" he shouted. "Wait up!"

She stopped dead in her tracks when she heard Greg's voice and turned around to wait for him. He trotted toward her and was slightly winded when he caught up to her.

"Are you okay?" he asked.

She walked toward him and embraced him before she buried her head in his chest. He slowly wrapped his arms around her, and then she broke down.

"It's gonna be okay, Roz," he said. "Jessica and I are here for you if you need us."

"It's not fair," she said, crying. "It's just not fair."

Greg continued to comfort her for several minutes before she gathered herself, and they entered the hospital through the emergency shortly afterwards. The clerk at the information desk gave them both hall passes and directed them to Ramona's room. Everyone was there by Ramona's bedside, including Horace, when they got to the room.

"Hey, Horace," Greg said as he gave him hug and firm handshake. "When did you get here?"

"Not long before you all," Horace answered. "Hey, Roz."

"Hi, Horace," Rosalyn said, hugging Horace tightly.

"How's she doing, Sasha?" Greg asked, giving her a warm embrace.

"Not good, Greg," Sasha answered. "She's not breathing on her own, and her organs are starting to shut down. She won't make it through the night."

"Damn, I'm sorry to hear that," Greg said.

"If you need anything, Sasha, I'm here for you," Rosalyn said.

"That goes for all of us," Jessica added.

"Thank you all," Sasha said.

"Anybody want something to drink?" Greg asked.

"No, thank you, baby," Pamela answered, and Rosalyn frowned after her reply.

"I'm good," Horace said.

"Can you bring me back a water?" Jessica asked.

"Sure, no problem," Greg answered. "Roz? Sasha?"

"No, thank you," Rosalyn answered.

"Nothing for me, either," Sasha answered.

"Okay, I'll be right back," Greg said.

"I'll walk with you," Horace said.

The two of them left the room, and Horace said, "Sasha's not dealing with this too well."

"I wouldn't expect her to be okay in a situation like this," Greg said. "Ramona is like a sister to her, and you rarely saw one without the other back in the day."

"I think we're gonna have to postpone the wedding to deal with this."

"You're probably right."

They found the vending machine shortly afterwards, and Greg bought a Pepsi and a water for Jessica. They stood there and continued their conservation instead of heading back to the room.

"It's crazy seeing Ramona on a respirator like that," Greg said. "I still can't wrap my mind around this."

"I know, and I feel kind of guilty because I judged her for not responding to our invitation," Horace said. "Now we know why."

"Don't feel bad about that—you had no way of knowing that she was sick, man."

"We heard about the robbery and shooting from Jessica, but she didn't really get into it," Horace said, changing the subject. "She just wanted to let Sasha and me know what was going on but didn't want to talk about it because of the current situation."

"Yeah, man, it was crazy," Greg said. "They made us strip down to our underwear and took people's wallets, purses, jewelry, and cell phones."

"*Uptown Saturday Night* style, huh?"

"Exactly."

"Man, that's jacked up. How much did they get you for?"

"Just my watch. They told everybody to toss their stuff in a pile after we stripped, but I left my phone, keys, and wallet in my pocket."

"Smart."

"If they wanted the rest of my stuff, they were gonna have to rummage through my pockets to get it."

"Yeah, every time we try to take two steps forward, something or somebody knocks you ten steps back. These punks need to be put down like rabid dogs."

"Indeed they do."

They walked back to the room only to find out that Ramona had flatlined. Sasha and Rosalyn wept in each other's arms, and Pamela and Jessica were failing to hold back their own tears.

"I'm so sorry, baby," Horace said to Sasha, and she let go her embrace from Rosalyn and buried her face in Horace's chest.

Greg put his arms around Pamela, and Jessica walked toward Rosalyn and embraced her.

"I'm here for you, Roz," Jessica whispered.

"Thank you, Jessica," Rosalyn said.

17

Greg and Pamela were on their way back from Ramona's funeral in Fayetteville, North Carolina, on a Saturday evening. Sasha's family had a slight delay in making the arrangements for Ramona due to issues with the funeral home because she had no insurance, but they were still able to bury her in two weeks' time. Greg came off the Interstate at the halfway point of the trip in Columbia, South Carolina for gas and to get something eat. There was a Wing Stop restaurant a mile or so off of Interstate 20, so they decided to eat there and get gas afterwards. Greg parked in the lot, and they went inside to order.

"What do you want to order?" Greg asked.

"I can get a six-piece wing combo," Pamela answered.

"Are you ready to order?" the cashier asked.

"Yes, let me get two six-piece wing combos, please," Greg answered.

"Classic or boneless?" the cashier asked.

"Classic for me," Greg answered.

"Classic," Pamela answered.

"What flavors do you want?" the cashier asked.

"I'll have the lemon pepper wings," Greg answered, "and what flavor do you want, Pam?"

"I'll have the Cajun wings," Pam answered.

"And what are your drinks?" the cashier asked.

"Coke for me," Greg answered.

"Coke, no ice," Pamela answered.

"It will be a fifteen-minute wait, and your total is $20.78," the cashier said.

Greg handed the cashier the exact amount, and they sat down in the dining area afterwards. He looked at watch and said, "We're making good time, but I'm starting to get tired."

"Me, too," she said. "We've been up since three o'clock this morning."

"Yeah, we had to leave early to make it the funeral by eleven."

"It was a nice service, wasn't it?"

"Yes, it was. The family put a nice photo of Ramona on the obituary."

"Mm-hmm. I noticed the Ramona and Sasha have the same last name—are they cousins or sisters? I don't know them that well and couldn't remember how they were related."

"They're first cousins. Ramona's mom died in a car crash when she was seven years old, so they were both raised by Sasha's mom."

"That's so sad."

"I know. Jessie and I lost our father to cancer when she was ten, and I was nine."

"Jessica's older than you, huh? I always thought you were the oldest."

"We're eleven months apart, but we graduated from grammar school and high school in the same year. Her birthday is in February, and mine is in December."

"I thought the cutoff date for birthdays in each grade was September…"

"I guess it depends on what school district you're in—my mom was able to get us in together."

"I'm sorry about your dad—I've only seen my dad a few times when I was really young, and I haven't seen him since then."

"Are you an only child?"

"No, I have a brother and a sister, and their dad married my mom. I consider him my dad because he helped raise me, too."

"It's good that you had a male role model in your life—my uncles picked up the slack when my dad passed away, so that Jessie and I didn't miss a beat."

"That's great."

Greg paused and said, "Ramona didn't look like herself—the cancer really took a toll on her."

"Yeah, she lost a lot of weight," Pamela said.

"Sasha seemed to keep it together really well, but I know Ramona's death hit her hard."

"Indeed. Rosalyn didn't take it well at all, though."

"It's understandable, because Ramona was her best friend. I'm just glad my sister is there for her to lean on."

"Me, too, because I don't want her trying to lean on you for comfort."

"Trust me; you have nothing to worry about in regard to Rosalyn."

"That's good to know."

Moments later, the cashier informed them that the food was ready, and Greg went to the counter to get their tray. He then placed their tray on the table, sat next to Pamela, and leaned into her for a kiss.

"I love it when you kiss me spontaneously," she said.

"And I love that you let me kiss you spontaneously," he said. "These last two weeks have been incredible, Pam. It feels so good to be desired by someone again."

"The last two weeks have been incredible for me, too, and you're desired very much by me—thank you for letting me ride with you to the funeral."

"Thank you for accompanying me because I hate traveling alone."

"Are you planning on driving all the way home tonight?" she asked, before taking a bite of a chicken wing.

"I don't know if I should," he answered. "It's starting to get dark outside."

"Maybe we should get a room."

"Yeah, that's a good idea. I don't want us to end up in a ditch or worse."

"So, what's next, now that you passed the CPA exam?" she asked, changing the subject. "I'm so proud of you."

"I got a job offer from BDO USA, and I'm going to accept it," he answered. "I have to work in the accounting field for a year before I can become a licensed CPA."

"That's great, Greg."

He ate a couple of fries before saying, "Thank you for supporting and encouraging me before my test last week."

"You can always count on me to support you, Greg," she said.

"I'm crazy about you, Pam."

"What did you say?"

"I said that I'm crazy about you. My feelings keep getting stronger and stronger each day that I spend with you."

"Wow, I didn't expect to hear that from you."

"Why?"

"I know that you just broke up with Jennifer, and you wanted to take things slow…"

"I know, but I feel so comfortable with you. You and I fit together."

"Yes, we do fit together. I'm so in love with you that it hurts—it hurts that I can't hold you in my arms every night, and it hurts that I haven't made love to you yet."

She began caressing his hand and arm as they glazed into each other's eyes. They finished eating their food and left the restaurant in search of a hotel to book. There was a Best Western off Bush River Road, so they booked a room there. After that, they wasted no time hugging, caressing, kissing, and disrobing each other.

"I want you so bad," she said.

"I want you, too," he said.

His smooth, caramel skin and chiseled six-foot-two-inch frame turned her completely on, and she was mesmerized by the fact that he was also well-endowed. He was captivated by her as well—her flawless and radiant chocolate skin, her voluptuous body and alluring sex appeal had him enthralled in her beauty. He laid her down on the bed ever so gently, and they made hot and passionate love to the point of total exhaustion. They then lay blissfully in each other's arms afterwards.

"You were absolutely incredible, baby," she said, kissing him on the lips.

"So were you," he said. "You're everything I've envisioned and more."

"I love you, Greg."

"I love you, too, Pam. I didn't think I could fall so quickly, but I did. My heart belongs to you now."

"And my heart belongs to you."

There was brief silence, and she asked, "So, do you think Horace and Sasha are still getting married?"

"I don't know," he answered. "Horace didn't make mention of a revised date, and I felt that it was inappropriate to ask him about it."

"Yeah, you're right. I hope that there's still a wedding in spite of the circumstances."

"Horace will be by Sasha's side every step of the way, and I'm certain that they will figure it out."

"I'm sure they will, too. Their relationship is so strong, and their example gives us all hope in a 'happily ever after' ending."

"Indeed it does, baby."

"Do you think we'll have a 'happily ever after' ending?"

"I sincerely hope so."

"I promise to be here for you through thick and thin. You make me so happy."

"And you make very happy as well. Thank you for restoring my trust in relationships."

"No, thank you, Greg. I didn't think I'd ever be this happy again, but you proved me wrong."

She leaned into him and kissed him passionately. They were back at it again before long and continued to make love until the wee hours of the morning.

18

"Do you need anything else, Ms. Mays?" Horace asked.

"No, baby, you've done more than enough already," Ms. Mays answered. "You have been a godsend to us."

"Do you know where Sasha is?"

"No, I haven't seen her since all the guests left the house earlier."

"I'll check the backyard...maybe she needed some alone time."

"Okay. I'll finish cleaning up the kitchen."

Horace stepped out the back door and onto the porch. The Mays residence had a huge backyard where a good portion of the guests from the funeral congregated—mostly family and friends from the Fayetteville area and a few of Ramona and Sasha's friends from college—most notably Greg. Jessica, Rosalyn, and Pamela. He sat down in one of the lawn chairs in the yard, and that was when he noticed Ms. Mays' car was gone. Maybe she needed to take a drive to clear her head, he thought. She had kept herself busy the entire day from the wake, funeral, burial, and reception; and she hadn't talked a whole lot during the course of the day. In fact, she'd never even shed a tear at the funeral or burial and hadn't had time to process everything yet.

Horace had paid the cost of everything because the family didn't have the money to pay the funeral home, and he'd paid a caterer for the food. He began to reflect on Sasha's bizarre behavior during the burial, and how Sasha showed no emotion when the casket was lowered into the ground. Rosalyn became hysterical and had to be held up by one of Sasha and Ramona's male cousins, but Sasha still showed no emotion and looked off into the distance as if she were preoccupied with something else other than the funeral.

Horace went back inside the house after ten minutes or so, and Ms. Mays was in the living room watching television. He sat across from her and said, "Sasha took your car for a drive to clear her head, I think."

"I figured as much," she said.

"So, she does this sort of thing a lot?"

"Yeah, when Sasha and Ramona were younger, like the time when they first entered high school, Sasha would disappear for hours after I would scold her for not doing her chores, or when Sasha and Ramona would have a major disagreement. She's always been a deep thinker and going somewhere to be alone and clear her mind was her way of coping with her issues."

"So, there's nothing to worry about?"

"No, she'll be fine."

"But did she seem kind of off to you, Ms. Mays? I mean, she didn't even cry when they lowered the casket into the ground."

"That's just her way, baby. She didn't cry when she was a little girl at Ramona's mother's funeral, and she didn't cry at her father's funeral a few years ago. She doesn't like to wear her emotions on her sleeve, but once she processes everything, she'll break down in her own quiet and private time."

"I see. Well, I'm going to wait for her to come home on the front porch, okay?"

"Okay, baby."

19

Tameka Snow was on her way home from Sunday morning service, and she had decided to stop at a Walgreens to pick up a few personal items. She was the type of woman whose sole purpose for going to church was to find a husband and who would pray to God for one every chance she got. She was also very beautiful—a five-foot-five, caramel-complected socialite who had a successful career as chemical engineer but felt that the only thing missing was the man of her dreams.

She was originally in the running for the Greg O'Brien sweepstakes after Rosalyn broke up with him at the end of their junior year at Clark, but she gave up once Jennifer snagged him weeks later. After Pamela hooked up with him two weeks ago, she was furious but didn't show it, and she was devastated once she found out that they were now a couple.

Eye shadow was on her list of things to buy, and coincidentally, Jennifer Mason was in the cosmetics aisle when she got there. There was no love lost between them, and they haven't seen or spoken to one another in over two years.

Jennifer had turned toward Tameka and waited for her to come where she was standing. They embraced moments afterwards, and Tameka said, "Long time, no see. No hard feelings, I hope."

"It's okay, girl," Jennifer said. "I'm long over it."

"I didn't mean to disrespect you at Sasha and Horace's engagement party back then. I was drunk and didn't mean to push up on Greg like that."

"It was a long time ago, and like I said, I'm over it. So, how have you been, Meka?"

"I've been good, Jen, thanks for asking. My pastor preached a great sermon this morning, and I'm just picking up a few items before I head on home."

"That's good. I've got a few errands to run myself on my only day off."

"Your firm has you working six days a week?"

"Yeah, I just got a huge promotion, and I have to stay on top of my game."

"That's great, girl."

Jennifer paused briefly and said, "I guess you heard about Greg and me."

"Yeah, Pam told me. Sorry."

"Don't be...I'm okay."

"I heard about what happened between you and Pam, and I'm very sorry about that, too."

Jennifer paused again and said, "I have to admit that I may have wrong about the whole situation, though. She gave it to me straight, but I couldn't handle the truth. Now, I don't have any real friends left."

"She might've told you the truth about you and Greg, but she really hasn't been a real friend to you, Jen."

"Why do you think that, Meka?"

"You obviously don't know, do you?"

"Know what, girl?"

"Pam tells me everything that goes on in her sordid little life, and let's just say that she didn't waste any time pushing up on Greg after you two broke up."

"Oh, really?"

"Yep. They went out to dinner and went to that hot new spot in Buckhead the same night it got robbed."

Jennifer was in deep thought after Tameka dropped that bombshell on her, and Jennifer finally said, "Pam can have Greg because I'm done with him, and he's her problem now."

"She also told me that Greg passed his CPA exam..."

Jennifer's heart sank when Tameka revealed the last tidbit of information, and a tear rolled down her cheek afterwards. Tameka put her arm around her and solemnly said, "It's going to be okay, Jen, and I'm here for you if you need me. You still have one true friend left."

"Thank you," Jennifer said, wiping the tears from her eyes. "I can't believe this is happening to me."

"Just so you know, I really went in on Pam and told her about herself right before she went to Ramona's funeral with Greg Friday..."

"Ramona's funeral? She's dead?"

"Yes, she died of cancer two weeks ago. Sasha didn't tell you?"

"No, I haven't spoken to Sasha in weeks. Damn, where have I been?"

"You cut us all off, Jen. We still love you and want to be a part of your life, but you get so angry and kick us all to the curb."

"I know—I'm sorry. I feel so horrible about this."

"Come here, girl."

Tameka embraced Jennifer as she began to sob uncontrollably, and they stood in the cosmetics aisle for seemingly an eon. Jennifer finally let go of her embrace and said, "I need help, Meka."

"Okay, sis, anything you need, I got you," Tameka said.

"No, you don't understand."

"Understand what?"

"I have a serious substance abuse problem that I can't seem to kick."

"What kind of substance abuse problem, Jen?"

"Cocaine, Meka. I start using it to keep me alert because I was putting in so many hours at the firm so that I could get this promotion, but now I'm hooked. What am I gonna do?"

"Relax, Jen. I'm sure that your firm has an anonymous hotline for drug or alcohol abuse, as most companies have treatment programs, and we can get you squared away on Monday so that you don't lose your job."

"What if the partners find out?"

"They won't—just take an FMLA so that you can receive the treatment you need. I'll be with you every step of the way, Jen. I love you."

"I love you, too, Meka. Thank you."

"No problem, girl. Come on, let's check out and get something to eat."

"Okay, that's sounds good to me."

20

It was almost noon, and Greg and Pamela were in Jessica's guest room lying in bed. Greg rolled over and look at his watch and sighed. Pam then yawned and stretched her arms.

"What time is it?" she asked.

"Almost noon," he answered.

"I smell food, and I'm starving."

"Me, too. Come on; let's see what Jessica is cooking."

"Okay."

They quickly got dressed and went into the living area of Jessica's apartment. Jessica had just finished whipping some breakfast up, and she said, "The dead have finally awakened. There's plenty of food here so help yourselves."

"Thank you, Jessica," Pam said.

"Yeah, thanks, sis," Greg added. "Smells great."

The three of them made their plates, and Greg got the orange juice and milk out the fridge. They wasted no time eating as everyone was famished.

"What time did you all get in this morning?" Jessica asked as she poured herself a glass of orange juice.

"About seven," Greg answered. "We wanted to get an early start this morning because we were supposed to go the nine-thirty service, but we crashed again once we got here instead."

"Y'all can miss me with Sunday service," Jessica said. "I'll be damned if I let these pastors pimp me out of my money."

"I feel you on that, sis, but there's more to church than just paying tithes and offerings," Greg said.

"Yeah, Jessica, this pastor is really good," Pamela added.

"I'll let y'all have that," Jessica said.

"Have you spoken to Sasha since the funeral?" Pamela asked Jessica, changing the subject.

"No, I haven't," Jessica answered.

"She didn't show any emotion, and I found that kinda strange," Greg said. "I guess I expected her to react more like Roz."

"Yeah, me too," Jessica said.

"What did Horace have to say about her behavior?" Pamela asked Greg.

"Nothing really," Greg answered. "He was pretty shook up himself."

"Right," Pam said. "Did he have a thing with Ramona before Sasha?"

"Who told you that?" Jessica asked, seemingly annoyed.

"I'm just saying that I heard rumors about them, that's all," Pamela answered.

"They had a one-night stand the semester before Horace started dating Sasha," Greg stated. "He didn't know that they were cousins at the time."

"Oh, okay," Pamela said.

They all finished eating around the same time, and Pam got up from the table and said, "I'm gonna freshen up a bit, baby."

"Okay," Greg said, kissing her on the lips.

Pamela went to the bathroom, and Jessica shook her head.

"What's that look for?" Greg asked.

"Because your girl is a trip, Greg," Jessica answered.

"Why you say that?"

"Don't you think what she said about Ramona and Horace was inappropriate?"

"Aw, sis, she didn't mean anything by it."

"She's messy—all I'm saying is be careful."

"You have nothing to be concerned about."

"So, you and Pam are really a couple now," Jessica stated. "Don't you care how this all looks?"

"How does what look, Jessie?"

"Pam was Jen's best friend. You can have any girl you want, but you picked Pam. This isn't a good look."

"Was it a good look when Jen hooked up with her married boss, sis? She brought that dude to our home, man."

"I know what she did was jacked up, but you don't have to stoop to her level. You know Roz and Jen are gonna start trippin' once they find out that y'all are a couple."

"Look, I couldn't care less how this looks, and can't care less about how Jennifer or Rosalyn feel about it. I'm done being a doormat for either one of them, and if they can't accept that Pam and I are together, too damn bad."

"I'm not trying to bust your balls, Greg…"

"I'm a big boy, sis…I can handle myself."

"I know you can handle yourself, but as the saying goes, *the same way you get someone is the same way you will lose them.*"

"So, what are you saying, huh? Pam's gonna get bored with me and go for another guy with deeper pockets?"

"I'm not saying anything else, Greg. It's your life."

"Damn right it's my life."

"Congrats on passing the CPA exam by the way."

"Thanks…it took you long enough to say something."

"I'm sorry. You know how busy I've been with work and the funeral."

"I know, Jessie, don't even take what I said seriously."

"When is your last day at McDonald's?"

"My last day was this past Thursday. I got a job offer with BDO, and I start November 1st."

"That's wonderful, Greg."

There was a buzz of the doorbell, and Jessica got up to answer it.

"Who is it?" Jessica asked.

"It's Roz," she answered.

"Damn," Greg said.

"Don't start backpedaling now," Jessica said. "You had to know that y'all were gonna run into her eventually."

"Better later than sooner," Greg said.

Rosalyn opened the door and said, "Hey, you two."

"Hey, Roz," Greg said.

"Hi, Greg," Rosalyn said.

Jessica hugged Rosalyn and said, "Help yourself to some breakfast before it gets cold."

"Don't mind if I do," Rosalyn said.

"When did you get back?" Jessica asked.

"Late last night," Rosalyn answered. "I think it was close to midnight."

"Have you spoken to Sasha?" Greg asked.

"Not since the funeral," Rosalyn answered.

"Did she seem a little off to you?" Greg asked.

"Sasha was just being Sasha," Rosalyn answered. "I guess that's her way of dealing with it, you know. I don't think it's really hit her yet."

"You're probably right," Greg said.

Pamela finally came out the bathroom with her hair and makeup intact. Rosalyn had a look of utter shock on her face.

"Hey, Rosalyn," Pamela said.

"Pamela," Rosalyn said. "What are you doing here?"

"I'm with Greg," Pamela answered.

"I see," Rosalyn said. "I originally came by to see if you wanted to go shopping with me, Jessie."

"Sure, let's do it," Jessica said.

Jessica cleared the kitchen table and said, "Can you wash the dishes for me, Greg?"

"Yeah, I got you," Greg answered.

"Well, I guess I'll see you guys later, then," Jessica said.

"See you later, sis," Greg said. "Bye, Roz,"

"Bye, Greg," Rosalyn said. "Pamela."

Pamela nodded at her as Rosalyn shut the door behind her. Greg turned to face Pamela and asked, "No love lost between you two, huh?"

"I'm not trippin' on her," Pamela answered.

"What do you want to do today?"

"Nothing really. I can relax and snuggle up to you all day."

"Whatever you want, baby."

21

Rosalyn and Jessica were on their way to Lennox Square, an upscale mall in Buckhead about a half-hour away from Jessica's place. Rosalyn figured that retail therapy would keep her mind occupied so that she wouldn't focus on Ramona.

"You showed incredible restraint, Roz," Jessica said. "I just knew that you were gonna go in on Pam once she came out the bathroom."

"She's not worth it, girl," Rosalyn said. "Besides, Greg and Pam are temporary because she's all wrong for him."

"You really should let that go."

"It's not even about me. Greg and I probably won't ever get back together, and I've come to terms with that reality. However, I still want what's best for him, and she ain't it."

"I agree with you there. Can you believe that she had the nerve to bring up that Ramona and Horace slept together while we were eating breakfast?"

"Really? Well, she's the type of classless chick who would say something crass like that. Greg will see her for what she truly is one day."

"I hope that one day is soon."

Jessica sighed and asked, "How are you holding up?"

"Not good, Jessie," Rosalyn answered. "I cried all night until I had no tears left. I figure that if I keep busy, the thought of Ramona won't consume my mind."

"I know, girl—it's really tough to wrap my mind around the fact that she's gone forever. However, you still got Sasha, and you still got me."

"Sasha and I are cool, but I'm not as tight with her as I was with Ramona."

"That's okay, Roz. You two are gonna need each other more now that Ramona is gone. Besides, I'm not holding you hand every damn day."

"You got jokes, huh?"

"I know you're needy as hell."

"Whatever."

"On a serious note, you know you can come to me for anything."

"I know—thank you."

"You're welcome."

Rosalyn parked in the garage on the side where Macy's was, and they went through the Macy's entrance. Rosalyn wanted to check out some bags and purses, so that was their first order of business.

"Which bag are you specifically looking for?" Jessica asked.

"I don't know," Rosalyn answered. "Whatever catches my eye, I guess."

"That chocolate Coach bag looks nice, or maybe you should get that Dooney & Bourke over there…"

Rosalyn sighed and said, "What the hell am I doing here? I don't want any of this stuff."

"It's all right," Jessica said. "We don't have to shop if you don't want to. We can do whatever you want to do."

Rosalyn wiped a tear from her eye, and Jessica said, "It's gonna take some time to get over this pain. It took me almost two years to get over the death of my father, so there's no time frame on how long a person is supposed to grieve."

"I have to do something, or else I'm gonna go crazy. Sitting at home sulking isn't an option."

"The only thing that's gonna get us through this is prayer, Roz. Pray every day until your pain becomes bearable."

"I'm not really into that, Jessie—you know—the whole church thing."

"I'm not big on church, either, but I have my own relationship with God. I try to live as righteously as I possibly can."

"You—righteous?"

"I know I'm not your typical Christian, but I do read the Bible quite often. Greg and I grew up in the church, but I no longer attend on a regular basis."

"Well, maybe I'll give God a try."

"Maybe you should."

22

Horace was watching television while lying in Sasha's old bed, and Sasha was still sleep as the clock read twelve twenty-two in the afternoon. Ms. Mays had gone to church earlier that morning, so they had the house to themselves. Sasha had come back home late last night when both Horace and Ms. Mays were sleeping and didn't alert either one of them to her presence.

The Carolina Panthers were playing the Steelers, and Horace appeared to be disinterested in the game as he was trying to figure out a way to talk to Sasha about their future plans without making her feel uncomfortable. He had adjusted his position in the bed, and this awakened her. He then greeted her, and she waved at him as she motioned to the bathroom. She returned to the bedroom moments later, and he sat up in the bed so that he could talk to her.

"How did you sleep?" he asked.

"Not good," she replied. "I tossed and turned all night long."

"What time did you get back?"

"I don't know—I guess around one in the morning."

"You could've let me know that you were leaving—you had me worried about you."

"Sorry, I just needed to be alone to clear my head of some things."

"Look, I know that the death of Ramona has taken its toll on all of us, but I have to move to New York sometime this week so that I can start at my dad's firm next week."

She paused briefly before saying, "I've thought long and hard about this, and I think that you should go to New York alone."

"Okay," he said. "I'll give you some more time to grieve Ramona and sort things out, and once I'm settled in our new apartment in New York, you can come and join me."

"I don't think you understand...I'm not moving to New York with you."

"Huh? You're right; I don't understand what you're saying to me."

"I want to stay here in Fayetteville, Horace. I need time to get myself together, and I don't feel like I can do that in New York."

"Take all the time that you need, baby. I'm not going anywhere."

"Maybe you shouldn't wait on me because I don't want to move to New York...ever."

He looked confused after her affirmation, and he finally asked, "You want to break up with me?"

"Yes, I need to be alone for a while. I'm stressed out with burying my cousin and planning this wedding. I need a break."

"We don't have to get married right this minute, Sasha. I just don't understand why you want to break up with me."

"I never wanted to follow you to Boston or New York, and I haven't been honest with you or myself."

"How come you never said anything?"

"Because I was caught up in the fact that you asked me to marry you, and I said yes because I love you. However, moving to Boston wasn't what I wanted to do, but I felt like following you was what I was supposed to do."

"Wow, I don't know what to say. I didn't know you felt that way because I would never try to force you to do something that you weren't prepared to do. I wish you had been honest with me..."

"Well, I'm being honest with you now, and moving to New York with you isn't an option for me. I'm sorry, Horace..."

"I'm sorry, too, Sasha. I guess I should leave now."

"Okay. Don't worry about packing my things...I'll fly to Boston and get my stuff when I feel up to it."

Horace nodded as he began packing his clothes in his suitcase. He then went to the bathroom to freshen up before calling himself an Uber to take him to the airport.

"I guess this is goodbye," he said. "I really wish you would reconsider your decision."

"My mind is made up," she said. "Goodbye, Horace."

"Goodbye, Sasha," he said, after he nodded at her with a grim look on his face.

Horace went outside, and the Uber driver was waiting patiently for him before he got out of the car to greet him and put his suitcase in the trunk. Sasha stood in the doorway as the Uber driver drove off, and Horace didn't look back when she waved at him.

23

One year later…

Druid Hills, Georgia, was the community that Greg and Pamela had chosen to buy their first home together. Greg had also gotten promoted to a new position at BDO USA once he completed his two thousand hour requirement to obtain his CPA license, and he received it via certified mail a week ago. Moving into their own home was a dream come true for both of them, and he had proposed to Pamela two months before his promotion. Their wedding was scheduled the Saturday after Thanksgiving.

It was a Saturday morning in mid-October, and both of them were exhausted from a long and stressful week of work. Greg had made some coffee with their brand new Keurig K200, and the aroma had awakened Pamela and led her to the kitchen.

"Good morning, baby," Pamela said.

"Hey, sweetheart," Greg said. "Want some coffee?"

"Yes, please."

Greg poured Pamela a cup of hazelnut coffee, and she took a sip of it and asked, "Did you mail the invitations yet?"

"I mailed them yesterday," he answered.

"Great. Are you excited about your new position?"

"It's a dream come true just like turning the key in the door of our home for the first time, and you saying yes when I proposed to you. None of this seems real to me yet."

"Me neither. Everything's falling into place for us."

"It's a shame that none of your soros will be at your wedding, though. So much for the so-called sisterhood."

"It's okay, baby. They're just little minions of Jennifer…she managed to turn them all against me by playing the victim…saying that I'm the reason that she couldn't get you back after she messed up. Tameka doesn't even speak to me anymore, either."

"Don't even worry about that. You don't need them anyway because you have me, and you have Jessie. Hell, Rosalyn has even warmed up to you somewhat."

"Yeah, she has, but only because she's found someone special and is deeply in love."

"Yeah, and that's great for her. I'm happy that Jessie agreed to be you maid of honor."

"Jessica's a lifesaver because my little sister Danielle couldn't do it. It's her last semester at Prairie View A&M, and she's taking her hardest classes needed to graduate with a degree in electrical engineering."

"She's still coming to the wedding, isn't she?"

"She wouldn't miss it for the world, in her exact words."

Greg paused and said, "Marriage is a monumental step in our lives—it's probably the most important decision that we'll ever make. Are you sure you're ready?"

"Yes, I am, Greg. The question is: are you ready? You're not getting cold feet on me, are you?"

"Absolutely not, Pam. I'm just saying, things between us have been great. Actually, they've been much better than great, but, we haven't weathered any storms yet. Do you think our relationship is strong enough to handle one?"

"Yes, I do. I feel that our love can withstand any obstacle placed in front of us."

"We talk a good game, but there are people out here who aren't happy for us. Jennifer has made it abundantly clear that she thinks you're not the woman for me, and that she could show me better than she could tell me. What the hell does that even mean? Does she know some deep, dark secret that you're not telling me?"

Pamela sighed and then answered, "Jennifer knows that I used to strip at Magic City freshman year because I couldn't afford my tuition. She thinks that she can hold it over my head so that I'll beg her not to tell you…"

"You were a stripper? Why didn't you tell me?"

"I'm telling you now…"

"But would you've told me if I didn't press the issue?"

"Yes, eventually, but I wasn't comfortable about telling you this yet."

"And the Sigmas still let you in their sorority?"

"I didn't tell Jennifer about it until months after I crossed over."

"Look, I'm not judging you because we all do what we have to do to survive in this life, but I have to ask the question…"

"I know where you're going with this, and the answer is *hell* no. I would never sleep with a guy for money."

"Well, I'm definitely relieved to hear that…"

"So, you don't want to get married now, huh?"

"What? Yes, of course I still want to marry you. I love you unconditionally, and I want you to be able to tell me anything. What you did in the past doesn't define who you are today, okay?"

"Okay."

"You know that I'm about ready to block Jen's damn number from her excessive calls and texts…it's funny how all of a sudden I matter to her now that I'm perfectly happy with someone else."

"I think I might have to pay Miss Thang a visit…"

"Don't even give her the satisfaction…she's just trying to get a rise out of you."

"We are going to get married next month and live happily ever after, so forget her."

"That's right…forget about her and anybody else who has a problem with us getting married."

"Is Horace still going to be your best man?" Pamela asked, changing the subject.

"As far as I know, yes," Greg answered.

"Has he talked to Sasha?"

"No, he said that he hadn't spoken to her in two months—their last conversation was when she got the rest of her things out of their apartment in Boston."

"That's so sad."

"Tell me about it. He still hasn't gotten over the whole situation, and he also told me that Sasha is seeing someone else in Fayetteville."

"Damn, that's terrible."

"So, can you understand my apprehension? I don't want what happened to them to happen to us..."

"And it won't, Greg. I promise."

They then kissed and embraced each other, and Greg pulled back and looked Pamela in the eyes before saying, "I can't wait to make you my wife, and I believe everything's gonna work out...you'll see."

"And I can't wait to be your wife and start our bland new life together. I love you, Greg."

"I love you, too. Come on, let's go out and get some breakfast."

24

The lease was up for Horace and Sasha's Cambridge apartment, and Horace drove to Boston to gather the rest of his belongings and take them back to New York. It was his first time back in Boston since he had moved the bulk of his stuff to his apartment in Manhattan at the beginning of the fall. He had renewed the lease last year, right before he passed the bar, and was hired by his father's firm, so they'd decided to keep the place for another year rather than break the lease or sublet the apartment. Keeping the place would've given them an excuse to get away from the hustle and bustle of New York on occasion. However, Ramona's death had completely altered their plans and changed the course of their entire lives.

Sasha had left all the photos that they had taken together, and she left the forty-two-inch HD television that was sitting in the living room area on a medium-sized table. Horace had some clothes, tools, the medium-sized table and law books to take back to New York, and he dumped the rest of the stuff that he didn't need. Sasha had already turned in her keys a couple of weeks ago, and Horace turned in his set of keys once he was done moving his things to his 2018 Ford Explorer.

Horace then decided to head over to Roxbury to get his hair cut by Raheem and catch up on what was going on in Boston since he was last there. The shop was crowded as usual for an early Saturday afternoon when he arrived, but this particular time he called ahead and scheduled an appointment.

"My man Horace," Raheem said. "Good to see you, brother."

"What's the good word?" Horace asked, giving Raheem a pound. "I see nothing has changed around here."

"You still got the best hand."

"Yeah, things are good for me at the firm, but my love life sucks right now."

"I'm sorry about that, man. Come on, lemme touch up that fade."

Horace sat down in Raheem's chair and said, "I'm just starting to get over being dumped, bro. She really had me messed up, because like I told you before; there were no warnings, no arguments or red flags…no nothing, bro."

"Yeah, I was shocked when you had told me about what happened. It was cold the way she played you."

"I don't know if I'd call what she did an act of betrayal, but she definitely caused me a lot of stress and pain."

"Come on, man, she got with another guy a month after y'all broke up," Raheem said before wrapping a towel around Horace's neck.

"It wasn't just another guy," Horace stated, "it was her high school sweetheart. I've had a long time to think about this, and the truth of the matter is Sasha is just a country girl at heart. Reacquainting with her ex was the safe choice for her."

"Why are you letting her off the hook so easily? Society tells us that a woman can do no wrong—but if the shoe were on the other foot, the backlash against you would've been ridiculous."

"This is true, but as men, we have to set the example—we can't sit around and wait for things to change in our favor. All I can do is put my faith in God and control my own behavior."

"I hear you, but I still say that what Sasha did was wrong, bro. Damn, you paid her cousin's funeral expenses, and then she dropped you like a hot potato afterwards."

"I did the right thing, Raheem…the family didn't have the money to bury Ramona, so I stepped up. I didn't just do it for Sasha."

"You're a better man than me, and I can admit that. I hope that Sasha knows what she had and comes to her senses."

"I can't dwell on that or wait around for her to come to her senses. I have to accept reality and move on."

"Now that's what I'm talking about, bro. There are way too many chicks out here to be stuck on stupid for just one of them."

Raheem had Horace touched up and ready to roll in about twenty minutes, and Horace paid him twenty for the cut and tipped him ten. Horace then looked at himself in the mirror and gave Raheem the thumbs up.

"Thanks, bro, I appreciate you," Raheem said. "Don't be a stranger."

"You're still my main barber," Horace said. "You're still see me at least once a month, unless I'm working a high-profile case."

"Say, speaking of cases, do you remember that guy George?"

"George who?"

"You know, the Malcolm X-looking dude who owns that youth organization…"

"Yeah, yeah…I remember him. What about him?"

"He caught a case in Atlanta last month and is sitting in Fulton County jail awaiting trial."

"Word?"

"Yeah, he was indicted for a murder that happened at some club last year…someone from his crew snitched on him to avoid a lengthy prison term."

"Damn, that's so messed up. I never would've guessed in a million years that he'd be the one who'd murder somebody."

"You just never know about some people."

"This is true. Well, I'm out, fam…see you next month."

"Peace, Horace."

25

It was almost two o'clock in the afternoon, and Jessica had been lounging around ever since she woke up in the late morning. She didn't feel like cooking breakfast like she had normally done when Greg was staying with her. She missed her brother, and the year that he lived there reminded her of when they had their first apartment together freshman year at Clark-Atlanta University. They used their Pell Grant overpayments to furnish the apartment and stock groceries, and they both had part-time jobs to maintain it.

She also didn't see much of Rosalyn these days, either, because her new man, Rodney Boone, kept her occupied most of the time. She enjoyed her success, but she was very lonely. Her cell phone rang, and she answered on the second ring.

"Hey, girl," Jessica said. "What you been up to?"

"Rodney had to work today, so I finally have some free time to myself," Rosalyn answered. "Wanna grab something to eat?"

"Yeah, that's cool. What you have a taste for?"

"Nothing in particular. I just miss hanging out with you."

"Don't let this guy occupy all your time, Roz. He ain't your husband yet."

"True, but we're still getting to know each other, you know. He's a great guy, and I love being with him."

"I'm not mad at you, girl, and I'm not hatin'. I wish I had what you have."

"And you will someday. You're beautiful, and you're smart...your Prince Charming is out there somewhere and will sweep you off your feet real soon because I can feel it."

"I hope you're right, Roz."

"Guess who I talked to yesterday," Rosalyn said, changing the subject.

"Who?" Jessica asked.

"Sasha called me out the blue, and we talked for a very long time."

"Yeah, how's she doing?"

"She's doing well, and she's engaged and has a baby on the way."

"Good for her..."

"You haven't spoken to her?"

"No, and I don't have any intentions of talking to her."

"So, you're Team Horace, huh?"

"What she did to him was foul, Roz, so I don't have anything to say to her."

"I felt that way, too, until I heard her side of the story..."

"Her side of the story? What could she possibly say to justify her actions?"

"Sasha felt that moving to Boston was a mistake...that if she were here in Atlanta, Ramona might still be alive. She thinks that not being here to look after Ramona and help with her treatments is the reason why she's dead."

"That's ludicrous, Roz. Sasha being here wouldn't have made much of a difference...it might have prolonged Ramona's life a few months, but her presence wouldn't have prevented the inevitable."

"She also couldn't marry Horace because she didn't fit into his world. She said that meeting his parents felt just like meeting the Obamas or something. She realized at that moment they were from two different worlds, and that things wouldn't work between the two of them."

"Okay, I get it, but why didn't she break it off with him after meeting his parents?"

"She was torn because she still loved Horace..."

"But she didn't love him enough to work through their issues. Look, women like Sasha are the reason why guys who have their stuff together like Horace don't take us seriously. She basically tossed him aside like he was worthless once she was done with him."

"I totally get what you're saying, but where's your sympathy for our girl? She was still mourning Ramona, and she probably made a rash decision..."

"That's your girl, Roz...I'm fresh out of sympathy for her, so we can agree to disagree on this."

"Okay."

Jessica's doorbell rang, and she said, "Someone's at my door. What time are you coming by?"

"Give me about an hour."

"Okay, see you then."

Jessica ended the call and buzzed the person in. Moments later, there was a knock at the door."

"Who is it?" Jessica asked.

"It's me, Jennifer," she answered.

Jessica unlocked her door and said, "You're the last person I expected to see. What do you want?"

"I want to talk to you about Greg and Pam," Jennifer answered.

"Come in and have a seat," Jessica said as she grabbed two bottles of water from the fridge and gave Jennifer one.

"Thank you," Jennifer said as Jessica handed her the water bottle.

"So, what about Greg and Pam?"

"He can't marry her."

"Why?"

"Because she's a whore. Did you know that she used to be a stripper?"

"Yeah, I knew that."

"And you're okay with your brother marrying a stripper?"

"It was a long time ago, and she was woman enough to come to me and tell me after Greg proposed to her."

"Does Greg know about her sordid past?"

"I'm sure that he does...Pam wanted Greg to hear it from her and not someone else."

"I can't believe you're on board with this, Jessica. Pam isn't the woman for him..."

"And you are? You dogged my brother out, and now you want to act like you care about what happens to him?"

"I'm very sorry about how things ended between Greg and me. I just want what's best for him."

"Pam is one of the best things that has ever happened to Greg, so you don't have to worry about him."

"Okay, if that's how you feel, then so be it. Don't say I didn't warn you."

"What does that mean, Jennifer?"

Jennifer got up from the sofa and said, "Goodbye, Jessica. Take care of yourself."

"Make this the last time you come by here," Jessica said curtly as she shut the door behind Jennifer.

"Damn, why do I keep befriending these phony women?" she asked herself.

26

Greg and Pamela had just finished grocery shopping after eating breakfast, and they were on their way home. They wanted to hurry up and unload the groceries, and then they were going to head back out the show to see the movie *Widows*. They hadn't a night out in weeks because they were consumed with finding a home to their liking and closing on it.

The entire process was somewhat stressful—the real estate agent was an arrogant, twentysomething woman who didn't fully understand or listen to their concerns, needs, and desires in purchasing their first home together; and this particular agent from hell made the home-buying experience harder than it had to be. The mortgage broker, on the other hand, was very considerate and patient. He was able to work around the fact that Greg's credit score was a little too low, or that Pamela didn't have enough income to qualify for a mortgage loan by herself, with some creative financing. The broker was able to somehow put her name of the loan alone because she had the higher score of the two of them, and he was able to use their combined income on the loan application. Greg had provided the earnest money for escrow and the down payment on the home, and the broker went well above and beyond the call of duty by finding a lender and working in conjunction with their real estate attorney to secure both of their names on the title of the home.

Greg parked his car in the driveway and opened the garage door. The garage was connected to the house, so they were able to unload the groceries without having to go through the front door, as the garage led directly to the kitchen.

"What time does the movie start?" Greg asked.

"It starts at three fifteen, but you know that we have a ten-minute grace period of new previews before the actual movie starts," Pamela answered.

"I hate getting there late…we're barely gonna have enough time to get some popcorn. Were you able to reserve us some seats in the back?"

"Yes, baby, I did. Relax, okay?"

"My bad, sweetheart. I barely have enough time during the week to complete every task I have assigned to me at work, and it's starting to spill over into my personal life."

"Well, welcome to the real world. It's only going to get more intense once we have children...this is only a preview of things to come."

"I know, and I'm up for the challenge."

"I'll grab the rest of the groceries so that you can freshen up...I'll go second because you're faster than me."

"Okay."

He quickly went upstairs to the bathroom to take a quick shower while she grabbed the final load of stuff from the car. She received a text from an unknown number after she placed the bags on the kitchen floor. She then unlocked her phone and looked at the text. It was a link to a YouTube video, so she clicked on it. The title of the video was *You Can't Turn A 'Ho Into A Housewife.*

Her curiosity was now starting to get the best of her, and a cold rush overcame her body as she anxiously pressed play. What she witnessed next completely mortified her. The video was old footage of a private bachelor party where she and another girl from the Magic City strip club had been hired to perform. She also noticed that the video had been posted yesterday, and that the video went viral, as it already received over one hundred thousand views after she watched it for about a minute or so. She dropped her phone and had begun wailing uncontrollably after she saw herself topless doing a split in front of the groom with her forty-inch legs. She then quickly grabbed her car keys off the kitchen counter and phone off the floor, and she abruptly left the house.

Greg was out the shower and fully dressed in about ten minutes, and he quickly ran downstairs to inform Pamela that he was out the bathroom. He looked toward the living room and kitchen area before shouting, "Pam! Come on, you need to get ready so that we can go!"

He then looked in the garage and saw that her car was gone. He pulled his phone out afterwards and dialed her number. Her phone went to voice mail after several rings.

"Where are you, baby?" he asked her. "Call me back."

27

Horace had just tipped the doorman fifty dollars for helping him unload his truck and bringing his belongings inside of his Manhattan apartment on the fourth floor at the corner of Central Park West and Eighty-Eighth Street. He was exhausted from the drive to and from Boston, and all that he had on his mind was to unwind with a Miller Draft.

The fact that he was truly alone had set in when turned in the keys to his Boston apartment earlier in the day. His heart felt hollow, and he tried his best to fight through the pain of being rejected by Sasha. He'd never gotten any real closure from their breakup, and he hadn't been able to move on and date someone else for fear of being rejected again. He was now a successful, eligible bachelor whose confidence in the opposite sex was completely shattered, and he was totally oblivious to the fact that his secretary and two associate attorneys had the hots for him.

He went to the kitchen to grab himself a beer, and then he turned on the television in the living room before sitting down on the sofa. Nothing remotely stirred his curiosity on the screen after flicking channels for a minute, so he settled on watching the movie *Barbershop* that had just begun. His mind really wasn't on watching the movie as he reflected on his career and his personal life instead, and he envisioned the next five years of his life and what he wanted to accomplish in that time frame. His original plan was to make partner in the first five years of being employed at his father's firm, and he wanted to be married to Sasha and have two children by then. However, his dream of marriage and children would be deferred.

He had finished half of his beer before he dozed off, and when he awakened, dusk had started to set in. He got up from the sofa to relieve his bladder. Then his phone rang. He rushed out the bathroom and saw that it was his father's number on the caller ID.

"Hey, Dad, what's up?" he asked.

"Hey, Son," Mr. Shingles said, "I need you to book a flight to Atlanta for Monday."

"Why?"

"I need you and Roy Haden to do an initial case analysis for a new client of ours."

"Who's the client?"

"His name is George Canty III; and he's being indicted…"

"For murder…I know."

"How did you know that?"

"I met George a year ago at Raheem's barbershop in Boston, and Raheem told me that he was indicted for murder earlier today. I had given George my card last year after we met."

"I see. Well, I arranged for Roy and you to sit down with him at the Fulton County jail tomorrow at one o'clock in the afternoon, so book the earliest flight possible."

"Okay, Dad. Will do. Talk to you in the morning."

"Okay, Son. Bye."

"Bye, Dad."

28

Tameka's doorbell rang, and she got up from the sofa to answer it. She had owned a home in the affluent Buckhead neighborhood that she purchased last spring. Tameka and Jennifer were thick as thieves again, after Tameka helped nurse Jennifer to recovery from her cocaine addiction. She was there to take Jennifer to her treatments and be the support system that she needed to overcome her ordeal. However, Jennifer might've kicked her drug habit, but the Jezebel spirit inside of her was still alive and well.

"Who is it?" she asked.

"It's me," Jennifer answered.

"Hey, girl," Tameka said as she unlocked the screen door to let her in. "Want something to drink? I have water, soda, or wine if you want something stronger."

"Let's crack open that bottle of wine, but only if you're going to drink some with me."

Tameka got two glasses and popped the cork of the bottle after saying, "Yeah, sure, I'll have a drink with you."

"Good, because we need to celebrate."

"What are we celebrating?"

"It's done," Jennifer said.

"What's done?"

"The video of Pam stripping at that private bachelor party, way back when we were freshmen, is on YouTube. My cousin Julia is good friends with the guy who recorded the video, and she got him to forward it to her. It truly is a small world."

"I don't know about this, Jen…"

"What do you mean you don't know about this?"

"I mean that you should just let sleeping dogs lie. Greg and Pam are happy, and you should've just left well enough alone."

"Greg cannot marry that tramp, Meka…whose side are you on, anyway?"

"You know I'm on your side, sis. I don't rock with Pam anymore."

"Act like it, then."

"I'm just saying…putting that video on YouTube isn't going to get Greg back."

"Maybe not, but at least Pam won't have him."

"Why do you care so much, huh? Greg has moved on, and so have you."

"I care so much because Pam stabbed me in the damn back, and I can't just let it slide."

"You have a great career, and you have great friends. You're also strong because you kicked your cocaine habit…you have a lot to be thankful for, so let this go, Jen."

"You're right; I have a lot to be thankful for, but I can't and won't let this go. I'm gonna make Pam pay…"

"Let's agree to disagree, okay?"

"Whatever, Meka."

"What's up with homecoming?" Tameka asked, shifting the gears of the conversation. "Are you going this year?"

"I'm going to try…it'll be good to see all the sisters. I really don't have time to talk to anyone these days besides you."

"Yeah, we should go this year. Who knows? Maybe we'll both meet Mr. Right."

"Okay, it's a date. Let's call everybody right now."

"Okay, let's do it."

A Personal Note of Thanks

Thank you for taking the time to purchase and read *Deception*. I would really love to hear from you, and it's customers like you who give me the inspiration to create urban fiction stories like this one. If you enjoyed reading the book, please leave an honest review at Amazon, and you can contact me for information about my current and upcoming books at: markstephenoneal@gmail.com

Made in the USA
Middletown, DE
24 November 2020

25117696R00070